Princess September and the Nightingale

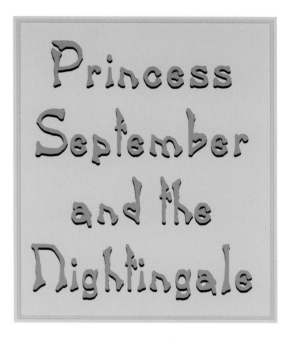

Princess September and the Nightingale

W. SOMERSET MAUGHAM

Illustrations by Richard C. Jones

Introduction by Jan Morris

Afterword by Samuel J. Rogal

Oxford University Press

New York · Oxford

Oxford University Press

Oxford   New York
Athens   Auckland   Bangkok   Bogotá   Bombay
Buenos Aires   Calcutta   Cape Town   Dar es Salaam   Delhi
Florence   Hong Kong   Istanbul   Karachi
Kuala Lumpur   Madras   Madrid   Melbourne
Mexico City   Nairobi   Paris   Singapore
Taipei   Tokyo   Toronto   Warsaw
and associated companies in
Berlin   Ibadan

"Princess September and the Nightingale" copyright © 1930
by Doubleday Doran & Co., Inc.
Renewed 1957 by W. Somerset Maugham
Introduction, Afterword, and illustrations copyright © 1998 by Oxford University Press, Inc.

"Princess September and the Nightingale" originally appeared in *The Gentleman in the Parlour*
(London: Heinemann; Garden City, N.Y.: Doubleday Doran & Co., 1930)

Published by Oxford University Press, Inc.
198 Madison Avenue, New York, New York 10016
Oxford is a registered trademark of Oxford University Press, Inc.

Library of Congress Cataloging-in-Publication Data
Maugham, W. Somerset (William Somerset), 1874–1965.
Princess September and the nightingale / W. Somerset Maugham;
illustrations by Richard C. Jones; introduction by Jan Morris;
afterword by Samuel J. Rogal.
p. cm.—(Iona and Peter Opie library of children's literature.)
ISBN 0-19-512480-4
[1. Fairy tales.]
I. Jones, Richard C., ill. II. Title. III. Series.
PZ8.M44879Pr   1998
[E]—dc21   98-9230
CIP
AC

1 3 5 7 9 8 6 4 2
Printed in Hong Kong
on acid-free paper

Introduction

JAN MORRIS

When this story was written, in 1922, the world seemed larger than it does nowadays. It took much longer then to get from one part to another, and not half so many people traveled abroad, so that the different nations of the planet knew far less about one another than they do today, in the age of the jet plane and TV satellite. Only the very rich went on holidays to exotic places far away; to most people the rest of the world was hardly more than a rumor, often exciting and tantalizing.

In particular, the peoples of the East and West thought of each other very differently in those days. Americans and Europeans were more advanced in technology, and generally much wealthier, so that Asians looked toward them with envy and admiration. On the other hand, Westerners tended to think of the Orient as somewhere mysteriously romantic, often holy—a place of gilded kings and peacocks, spices, silks, marble palaces and pagodas, scented temples, legends and fairy tales.

Many parts of the Orient had been, at one time or another, colonized and governed by Europeans, and this had slightly punctured the mystery of them—it was hard to be altogether spellbound by the reputation of a place if your Uncle Theodore had been a magistrate there, or if your Aunt Ethel never stopped talking about her childhood years on a coffee plantation in the tropics. One fascinatingly alluring country, though, had never been conquered, never become subject to one of the Western empires, and lived always in its own way, governed by its own kings, dancing its own elegant dances, worshiping its own gods in exquisite temples. It was called Siam then (we call it Thailand now), and by 1930 it remained entirely independent when all around it Asian peoples had fallen under the domination of the French, the British, or the Dutch. Its royal family lived in a cool and lovely palace beside the river in Bangkok, the capital, and to visitors from more ordinary countries its people always seemed to be smiling.

This was the place that Somerset Maugham, a novelist and playwright then at the peak of his fame, chose as the setting for *Princess September and the Nightingale.* It was not surprising. Maugham was as susceptible as most Westerners to the magic of the East, and he had been a traveler in those parts on and off for nearly 25 years. But he was a very worldly man, born in France of English parents, educated in England and in Germany. He was decidedly not sympathetic to the attitudes of the cruder colonial settlers, who often tended to view local cultures with contempt and did their best to remold local ways of life according to their own tastes. Siam was a country still gloriously itself, just the place to set a fairy tale whose heroine was a little Eastern princess with a nightingale for a friend.

I don't think we need to read profound meanings into the story—it is just a fairy tale, imbued with the sweet magic of its strange and foreign setting. But when we read it, moving with its narrative among the sunlit rooms of the royal palace, hearing the chatter of its nine princesses, the squawking of its parrots, and the tinkling of its temple bells, it is easy to imagine Mr. Maugham himself watching it all from a corner of the room, through a half-open door or a terrace window—a visitor from another world, bewitched by what he sees and fancies. Probably no Siamese could have written a story quite like this: for some of the light that floods through the story, like the delicate music that seems to sound through it, is the light of delighted astonishment.

Nowadays hundreds of thousands of Westerners go to Thailand for their vacations, and its life and art have become familiar everywhere in the world: in *Princess September and the Nightingale* we may still sense something of what it was like to arrive there as a visitor from the West 70 or 80 years ago, when all was still strange and wonderful. It is pleasant to know that Somerset Maugham, who grew to love the city of Bangkok, is still remembered fondly there in return: a suite is named for him to this day in the hotel beside the river where he used to stay, dreaming up stories perhaps, watching for kings to pass by outside, or listening for the nightingales.

Princess September and the Nightingale

Frst the King of Siam had two daughters, and he called them Night and Day. Then he had two more, so he changed the names of the first ones and called the four of them after the seasons, Spring and Autumn, Winter and Summer. But in course of time he had three others, and he changed their names again and called all seven by the days of the week. But when his eighth daughter was born he did not know what to do till he suddenly thought of the months of the year. The Queen said there were only twelve and it confused her to have to remember so many new names, but the King had a methodical mind and when he made it up he never could change it if he tried. He changed the names of all his daughters and called them January, February, March (though of course in Siamese), till he came to the youngest who was called August, and the next one was called September.

"That only leaves October, November and December," said the Queen. "And after that we shall have to begin all over again."

"No, we shan't," said the King, "because I think twelve daughters are enough for any man, and after the birth of dear little December I shall be reluctantly compelled to cut off your head."

He cried bitterly when he said this, for he was extremely fond of the Queen. Of course it made the Queen very uneasy, because she knew that it would distress the King very much if he had to cut off her head. And it would not be very nice for her. But it so happened that there was no need for either of them to worry, because September was the last daughter they ever had. The Queen only had sons after that, and they were called by the letters of the alphabet, so there was no cause for anxiety there for a long time, since she had only reached the letter J.

Now the King of Siam's daughters had had their characters permanently embittered by having to change their names in this way, and the older ones, whose names of course had been changed oftener than the others, had their characters more permanently embittered. But September, who had never known what it was to be called anything but September (except of course by her sisters, who because their characters were embittered called her all sorts of names) had a very sweet and charming nature.

The King of Siam had a habit which I think might be usefully imitated in Europe. Instead of receiving presents on his birthday he gave them, and it looks as though he liked it, for he used often to say he was sorry he had only been born on one day and so only had one birthday in the year.

But in this way he managed in course of time to give away all his wedding presents, and the loyal addresses which the mayors of the cities in Siam presented him with, and all his old crowns which had gone out of fashion.

One year on his birthday, not having anything else handy, he gave each of his daughters a beautiful green parrot in a beautiful golden cage. There were nine of them, and on each cage was written the name of the month which was the name of the princess it belonged to. The nine princesses were very proud of their parrots, and they spent an hour every day (for like their father they were of a methodical turn of mind) in teaching them to talk. Presently all the parrots could say God save the King (in Siamese, which is very difficult), and some of them could say Pretty Polly in no less than seven Oriental languages. But one day when the Princess September went

to say good morning to her parrot she found it lying dead at the bottom of its golden cage. She burst into a flood of tears, and nothing that her Maids of Honour could say comforted her. She cried so much that the Maids of Honour, not knowing what to do, told the Queen, and the Queen said it was stuff and nonsense and the child had better go to bed without any supper. The Maids of Honour wanted to go to a party, so they put the Princess September to bed as quickly as they could and left her by herself.

And while she lay in her bed, crying still, even though she felt rather hungry, she saw a little bird hop into her room. She took her thumb out of her mouth and sat up. Then the little bird began to sing, and he sang a beautiful song all about the lake in the King's garden, and the willow trees that looked at themselves in the still water, and the goldfish that glided in and out of the branches that were reflected in it. When he had finished the Princess was not crying any more and she quite forgot that she had had no supper.

"That was a very nice song," she said.

The little bird gave her a bow, for artists have naturally good manners, and they like to be appreciated.

"Would you care to have me instead of your parrot?" said the little bird. "It's true that I'm not so pretty to look at, but on the other hand I have a much better voice."

The Princess September clapped her hands with delight, and then the little bird hopped onto the end of her bed and sang her to sleep.

When she awoke next day the little bird was still sitting there, and as she opened her eyes he said, "Good morning." The Maids of Honour brought in her breakfast, and he ate rice out of her hand, and he had his bath in her saucer.  He drank out of it, too. The Maids of Honour said they didn't think it was very polite to drink one's bath water, but the Princess September said that was the artistic temperament. When he had finished his breakfast he began to sing again so beautifully that the Maids of Honour were quite surprised, for they had never heard anything like it, and the Princess September was very proud and happy.

"Now I want to show you to my eight sisters," said the Princess.

She stretched out the first finger of her right hand so that it served as a perch, and the little bird flew down and sat on it. Then, followed by her Maids of Honour, she went through the palace and called on each of the princesses in turn, starting with January, for she was mindful of etiquette, and going all the way down to August. And for each of the prin-

cesses the little bird sang a different song. But the parrots could only say God save the King and Pretty Polly. At last she shewed the little bird to the King and Queen. They were surprised and delighted.

"I knew I was right to send you to bed without any supper," said the Queen.

"This bird sings much better than the parrots," said the King.

"I should have thought you got quite tired of hearing people say, 'God save the King,'" said the Queen. "I can't think why those girls wanted to teach their parrots to say it too."

"The sentiment is admirable," said the King, "and I never mind how often I hear it. But I do get tired of hearing those parrots say, 'Pretty Polly.'"

"They say it in seven different languages," said the princesses.

"I dare say they do," said the King, "but it reminds me too much of my councillors. They say the same thing in seven different ways, and it never means anything in any way they say it."

The princesses, their characters as I have already said being naturally embittered, were vexed at this, and the parrots looked very glum indeed. But the Princess September ran through all the rooms of the palace, singing like a lark, while the little bird flew round and round her, singing like a nightingale, which indeed it was.

Things went on like this for several days, and then the eight princesses put their heads together. They went to September and sat down in a circle round her, hiding their feet as it is proper for Siamese princesses to do.

"My poor September," they said, "we are so sorry for the death of your beautiful parrot. It must be dreadful for you not to have a pet bird as we have. So we have put all our pocket money together, and we are going to buy you a lovely green and yellow parrot."

"Thank you for nothing," said September. (This was not very civil of her, but Siamese princesses are sometimes a little short with one another.) "I have a pet bird which sings the most charming songs to me, and I don't know what on earth I should do with a green and yellow parrot."

January sniffed, then February sniffed, then March sniffed; in fact all the princesses sniffed, but in their proper order of precedence. When they had finished September asked them:

"Why do you sniff? Have you all got colds in the head?"

"Well, my dear," they said, "it's absurd to talk of *your* bird when the little fellow flies in and out just as he likes." They looked round the room

and raised their eyebrows so high that their foreheads entirely disappeared.

"You'll get dreadful wrinkles," said September.

"Do you mind our asking where your bird is now ?" they said.

"He's gone to pay a visit to his father-in-law," said the Princess September.

"And what makes you think he'll come back ?" asked the princesses.

"He always does come back," said September.

"Well, my dear," said the eight princesses, "if you'll take our advice you won't run any risks like that. If he comes back, and mind you, if he does you'll be lucky, pop him into the cage and keep him there. That's the only way you can be sure of him."

"But I like to have him fly about the room," said the Princess September.

"Safety first," said her sisters ominously.

They got up and walked out of the room, shaking their heads, and they left September very uneasy. It seemed to her that her little bird was away a long time, and she could not think what he was doing. Something might have happened to him. What with hawks and men with snares you never knew what trouble he might get into. Besides, he might forget her, or he might take a fancy to somebody else, that would be dreadful; oh, she wished he were safely back again, and in the golden cage that stood there empty and ready. For when the Maids of Honour had buried the dead parrot they had left the cage in its old place.

Suddenly September heard a tweet-tweet just behind her ear, and she saw the little bird sitting on her shoulder. He had come in so quietly and alighted so softly that she had not heard him.

"I wondered what on earth had become of you," said the Princess.

"I thought you'd wonder that," said the little bird. "The fact is I very

nearly didn't come back tonight at all. My father-in-law was giving a party, and they all wanted me to stay, but I thought you'd be anxious."

Under the circumstances this was a very unfortunate remark for the little bird to make.

September felt her heart go thump, thump against her chest, and she made up her mind to take no more risks. She put up her hand and took hold of the bird. This he was quite used to, she liked feeling his heart go pit-a-pat, so fast, in the hollow of her hand, and I think he liked the soft warmth of her little hand. So the bird suspected nothing, and he was so surprised when she carried him over to the cage, popped him in, and shut the door on him that for a moment he could think of nothing to say. But in a moment or two he hopped up on the ivory perch and said:

"What is the joke?"

"There's no joke," said September, "but some of Mamma's cats are prowling about to-night, and I think you're much safer in there."

"I can't think why the Queen wants to have all those cats," said the little bird, rather crossly.

"Well, you see, they're very special cats," said the Princess, "they have blue eyes and a kink in their tails, and they're a specialty of the Royal Family, if you understand what I mean."

"Perfectly," said the little bird, "but why did you put me in this cage without saying anything about it? I don't think it's the sort of place I like."

"I shouldn't have slept a wink all night if I hadn't known you were safe."

"Well, just for this once I don't mind," said the little bird, "so long as you let me out in the morning."

He ate a very good supper and then began to sing. But in the middle of his song he stopped.

"I don't know what is the matter with me," he said, "but I don't feel like singing to-night."

"Very well," said September, "go to sleep instead."

So he put his head under his wing and in a minute was fast asleep. September went to sleep too. But when the dawn broke she was awakened by the little bird calling her at the top of his voice.

"Wake up, wake up," he said. "Open the door of this cage and let me out. I want to have a good fly while the dew is still on the ground."

"You're much better off where you are," said September. "You have a beautiful golden cage. It was made by the best workman in my papa's

kingdom, and my papa was so pleased with it that he cut off his head so that he should never make another."

"Let me out, let me out," said the little bird.

"You'll have three meals a day served by my Maids of Honour; you'll have nothing to worry you from morning till night, and you can sing to your heart's content."

"Let me out, let me out," said the little bird. And he tried to slip through the bars of the cage, but of course he couldn't, and he beat against the door, but of course he couldn't open it. Then the eight princesses came in, and looked at him. They told September she was very wise to take their advice. They said he would soon get used to the cage and in a few days would quite forget that he had ever been free. The little bird said nothing at all while they were there, but as soon as they were gone he began to cry again: "Let me out, let me out."

"Don't be such an old silly," said September. "I've only put you in the cage because I'm so fond of you. *I* know what's good for you much better than you do yourself. Sing me a little song and I'll give you a piece of brown sugar."

But the little bird stood in the corner of his cage, looking out at the blue sky, and never sang a note. He never sang all day.

"What's the good of sulking?" said September. "Why don't you sing and forget your troubles?"

"How can I sing?" answered the bird. "I want to see the trees and the lake and the green rice growing in the fields."

"If that's all you want I'll take you for a walk," said September.

She picked up the cage and went out, and she walked down to the lake

round which grew the willow trees, and she stood at the edge of the rice fields that stretched as far as the eye could see.

"I'll take you out every day," she said. "I love you and I only want to make you happy."

"It's not the same thing," said the little bird. "The rice fields and the lake and the willow trees look quite different when you see them through the bars of a cage."

So she brought him home again and gave him his supper. But he wouldn't eat a thing. The Princess was a little anxious at this, and asked her sisters what they thought about it.

"You must be firm," they said.

"But if he won't eat he'll die," she answered.

"That would be very ungrateful of him," they said. "He must know that you're only thinking of his own good. If he's obstinate and dies it'll serve him right, and you'll be well rid of him."

September didn't see how that was going to do *her* very much good, but they were eight to one and all older than she, so she said nothing.

"Perhaps he'll have got used to his cage by tomorrow," she said.

And next day when she awoke she cried out good-morning in a cheerful voice. She got no answer. She jumped out of bed and ran to the cage. She gave a startled cry, for there the little bird lay, at the bottom, on his side, with his eyes closed, and he looked as if he were dead. She opened the door and putting her hand in lifted him out. She gave a sob of relief for she felt that his little heart was beating still.

"Wake up, wake up, little bird," she said.

She began to cry and her tears fell on the little bird. He opened his eyes and felt that the bars of the cage were no longer round him.

"I cannot sing unless I'm free, and if I cannot sing I die," he said.

The Princess gave a great sob.

"Then take your freedom," she said. "I shut you in a golden cage because I loved you and wanted to have you all to myself. But I never knew it would kill you. Go. Fly away among the trees that are round the lake and fly over the green rice fields. I love you enough to let you be happy in your own way."

She threw open the window and gently placed the little bird on the sill. He shook himself a little.

"Come and go as you will, little bird," she said. "I will never put you in a cage any more."

"I will come because I love you, little princess," said the bird. "And I will sing you the loveliest songs I know. I shall go far away, but I shall always come back, and I shall never forget you." He gave himself another shake. "Good gracious me, how stiff I am," he said.

Then he opened his wings and flew right away into the blue. But the little princess burst into tears, for it is very difficult to put the happiness of someone you love before your own, and with her little bird far out of sight

she felt on a sudden very lonely. When her sisters knew what had happened they mocked her and said that the little bird would never return. But he did at last. And he sat on September's shoulder and ate out of her hand and sang her the beautiful songs he had learned while he was flying up and down the fair places of the world. September kept her window open day and night so that the little bird might come into her room whenever he felt inclined, and this was very good for her; so she grew extremely beautiful. And when she was old enough she married the King of Cambodia and was carried all the way to the city in which he lived on a white elephant. But her sisters never slept with their windows open, so they grew extremely ugly as well as disagreeable, and when the time

came to marry them off they were given away

to the King's councillors with

a pound of tea and

a Siamese

cat.

Afterword

SAMUEL J. ROGAL

Given the overall realistic, sometimes depressing, and occasionally sarcastic tenor of the fiction and drama of William Somerset Maugham (1874–1965), his *Princess September and the Nightingale* (1939) appears as something of a lighthearted anomaly. Certainly, Maugham, the consummate professional writer, would turn his pen in just about any creative direction that would generate the income necessary to sustain his expatriate patrician life-style. This was particularly true once he was installed at his Villa Mauresque on the French Riviera and traveling to Europe, North Africa, and Southeast Asia. In addition to *Princess September,* Maugham produced in 1939 a major novel *(Christmas Holiday)* and an anthology (with his critical preface) of 100 stories created by writers from the United States, Britain, France, Russia, and Germany *(Tellers of Tales)*. Nonetheless, to find Maugham's name within the usually fantasy-laden atmosphere of the juvenile literature of the 1920s and 1930s comes as somewhat of a surprise. Moreover, the circumstances by which the piece came into being reveal an especially interesting bibliographical process.

Maugham initially published, in the December 1922 issue of *Pearson's Magazine,* a short story (a fable, actually) entitled, simply, "Princess September." Then, in April 1924, the sponsors of the British Empire Exhibition of

1924–1925, at Wembley, invited Maugham (as they did playwright James Matthew Barrie, novelist Arnold Bennett, critic and fiction writer G. K. Chesterton, critical essayist and poet Edmund Gosse, and poet A. E. Houseman, among others) to transcribe the story, in his own handwriting, onto 53 pages of a one-inch high volume, with yellow calf binding and bearing Queen Mary's personal bookplate, as a contribution to the library of the Queen's Doll's House. That model, designed and built in 1923 (on a scale of one inch to the foot) for the exhibition by the noted architect Sir Edwin Landseer Lutyens, at a cost of approximately 200,000 British pounds (or 1 million U.S. dollars), represented a gift of the British people to King George V and Queen Mary. Lutyens had patterned his house after the original Marlborough House in London, designed by Sir Christopher Wren. As a result of its appearance there, Maugham's story naturally found its way into *The Book of the Queen's Doll House Library* (1924), edited by Edward Verrall Lucas (1868–1938), as well as Maugham's 1930 collection of his own short stories, *The Gentleman in the Parlour: A Record of a Journey from Rangoon to Haiphong.* It also appeared in the second volume of Maugham's 1952 *Complete Short Stories* (subtitled *The World Over*). Finally, in 1939, Oxford University Press converted the piece into a children's book under the title *Princess September and the Nightingale,* with color illustrations by one Richard C. Jones (born in 1910).

A native of Chicago, Jones spent his childhood there and in Lancaster, Pennsylvania, and he described his early work as "scribbles [that] were purely decorative design. This was not a matter of choice; it was my allotment. Born in an earlier period, I would have designed and decorated porcelains." In 1930, at age 19, Jones, with four dollars in his pocket and five complete sets of designs for five books, went to New York, where he received three immediate commissions. Unfortunately, the Great Depression caused an abrupt halt to advances for those commissions, reducing Jones to illustrating book jackets and title pages. "It was not until 1939," recalled Jones, "when Oxford University Press published my designs for Somerset Maugham's little Siamese fairy tale, *Princess September and the Nightingale,* that I felt any real pleasure for my published work." The Maugham book considerably elevated Jones's reputation as an illustrator, and he reached his pinnacle in 1951 with his pictures for *Planto-nio, the Pride of the Plain; A Ballad of the Old West; Retold and Illustrated by Dick Jones* (New York: Harcourt Brace and Company)—a "Night before Christmas" type of story of a western pony and how he and his rider saved a fort from hostile attackers.

Richard Jones was not the only person who failed to understand completely either *Princess September* or its creator, and he evidently concluded that Maugham concocted the piece as a "little Siamese fairy tale." Maugham's intentions, literary and otherwise, were not always immediately discernible. Consider, initially, the circumstances under which the story came into being. In late September 1922, Maugham and his secretary-companion, Gerald Haxton, embarked from London upon a nine-month tour of Burma, Siam, and Indochina—as always, to gather fresh material for Maugham's fiction and drama. Instinctively, Maugham favored the realistic atmosphere of "local color" in his work—whether it be the rocky coast of Kent or the teeming streets of Hong Kong. He particularly relied upon the people and places of the Near and Far East, with their stereotypical suggestions of the mysterious and the exotic, to authenticate his fictional and theatrical settings.

One of Maugham's primary concerns focused upon transplanted English men and women who went off (or who had been sent off) to various English colonies, who never would merge with or adapt to the cultures of those places, who instead insulated themselves in their clubs and government houses, and who almost always sent their children back to England for education. Such novels, short story collections, and plays as *The Explorer* (1908), *The Moon and Sixpence* (1919), *East of Suez* (1922), *Caesar's Wife* (1922), *The Letter* (1924, 1925), *The Painted Veil* (1925), *The Casuarina Tree* (1926), *The Sacred Flame* (1928), *The Narrow Corner* (1932), and *Ah King* (1933) all occur in lands traditionally considered exotic and "mysterious" because the British civil servants and company clerks never bothered to understand them. These works included local characters—servants, priests and worshipers, and assorted women—who performed a variety of stereotypical functions. Significantly, the principal characters tend to be Anglo-Saxon Britons (with an occasional transplanted American), while those "natives" of any fictional importance have been endowed with Eton and Oxford associations. For example, his 1922 play *East of Suez* opens with a lengthy and elaborate panorama of Chinese coolies, water carriers, rickshaws, and a caravan of Mongolian camels and Mongolian merchants. In the fourth scene, following an attempted assassination of a central character, Maugham floods the stage with a mob of Chinese monks and street people who come to view the wounded man. The constant and voluminous chatter in both scenes does indeed provide melodramatic tension, but really has no serious effect upon the movement or substance of the piece. Maugham simply pastes an Oriental setting behind a conventional Edwardian play in which a half-English, half-Chinese woman with a questionable past promises to marry (and does) one Englishman, but really loves another Englishman. In the seventh and final scene, the English lover kills himself and the English husband realizes that he has made a mistake to marry someone of another race; that marriage, according to Edwardian standards, was, from its outset, doomed to failure.

Certainly, the preceding patterns hold true for *Princess September.* Touring by car, boat, and raft, Maugham and Haxton journeyed to and through such places as Ceylon, Rangoon, the Tibetan border, Mandalay, and Bangkok, pausing at monasteries and government rest houses. At Bangkok, Maugham received an invitation to a night's sleep in the palace of the king of Siam, and there, because of his failure to take advantage of the mosquito netting supplied to him, he caught malaria. He spent almost a week in his hotel room, fighting a fever of 105 degrees, and during this enforced break in his travels he recast a recognizable Aesop fable ("The Nightingale and His Cage") into a short story entitled "Princess September." Seventeen years later, the critics of the sophisticated popular magazines came upon the illustrated Oxford edition of that story. The reviewer for the *New Yorker* concluded, simply and succinctly, "It is neatly told." However, the reviewer for *Books* appeared to have grasped the full intent of the new volume and, despite its mixture of Western thought and Eastern motif, recognized its potential to attract children: "When this story appeared in 'The Gentleman in the Parlour: A Record of a Journey from Rangoon to Haiphong,' Richard C. Jones wanted to give it illustrations worthy of this so charming a bit of Saimoiserie. He has now provided precisely the right pictures, large and small, brilliant in color, delicately humorous in design, and one of the most decorative picture books of the season results." Nonetheless, there are those who maintain that a number of subtleties and humorous fragments contribute to placing *Princess September* on an "adult" level as well, and thus a slight but fascinating critical dilemma arises.

The "adult" level upon which the story exists clearly divides into two parts. First, the nightingale, as singer, represents the artist as romantic free spirit. Placed in its cage, restricted by forces or elements over which it has no control, it will not create. "'I cannot sing unless I'm free and if I cannot sing, I die,' he said." Princess September, embracing the misguided advice from her methodical and noncreative sisters, tries to control the nightingale for herself, fearing that his passion for freedom will at some point take him away from her. Realizing, however, that his death would rob the world of true artistic expression, September releases him. "I love you enough to let you be happy in your own way." Herein lies the universal lesson applicable to children and adults.

As artist, Maugham recognized his connection to that nightingale. His temperament made him crave freedom. Although trained and licensed as a physician and surgeon since 1897, Maugham never practiced medicine—nor did he ever hold a "job" in the traditional, workaday meaning of that term. He devoted his entire adult life to writing, choosing never to be burdened by the vocational and social demands of the conventional workplace.

Second, the fable turned story also sounds political overtones, notes of irony easily recognizable to adults who read newspapers or history, but perhaps not totally appreciated by children unfamiliar with certain of the empty-headed nuances of government or of the purposes of political criticism. Maugham's king of Siam clearly possesses the qualities of the Western politician, particularly "a methodical mind," and "when he made it up he never could change it if he tried." His queen of Siam comes forth as a shallow creature, confused by having to remember so many new names for the children whom she continually bears. Still, the king and queen of Siam represent authority figures, and certainly young readers understand authority. The idiosyncrasies of those monarchs may arise from Maugham's eagerness to play political satirist, and the finer points of that satire may sail unnoticed over his young readers' heads. Nonetheless, attentive youngsters can hardly escape noticing a king and queen who (in A. E. Houseman's words) "Look into the pewter pot/To see the world as the world's not."

The piece deteriorates into music hall comedy when the king threatens to behead the queen should she bear more daughters beyond 12—and thus necessitate a new system for naming them. "But it so happened that there was no need for either of them to worry, because September was the last daughter they ever had. The Queen had only sons after that, and they were called by the letters of the alphabet, so there was no cause for anxiety there for a long time, since she had only reached the letter J." Then Maugham raises the issue of the king's birthday and the unaccustomed (in Europe) tradition of giving presents rather than receiving them. The cities of Siam claim mayors as their chief officials; the king's daughters teach their parrots to sing "God Save the King" in Siamese, a sentiment of which the king never tires of hearing; the king's councillors "say the same thing in seven different ways"; those same parrots can chant "Pretty Polly" in at least seven Oriental languages; the nightingale demonstrates his "artistic temperament" by drinking his bath water. Other than its setting in a far-off and imaginary court of Siam, wherein lie the romance and mysteries of Siamese culture? The writer tells us, parenthetically, that the king has named his daughters February through September, "though of course in Siamese"—as though suddenly remembering that Siam has its own language! However, for those familiar with Maugham's work, such rains of disappointment do not dampen the spirits. The resolution of such multicultural issues simply does not figure in this writer's fictional formula. Since Maugham's death on December 22, 1965, the very elements that brought him such popularity during the first four decades of the 20th century have not always found their mark upon the readers of the present generation. Those who continue to read Maugham do so because of his craft as a writer of fiction and drama; they need not always pay close attention to his substance.

Princess September and the Nightingale cannot be completely dismissed as a children's story. The argument over whether Maugham did or did not intend *Princess September* for young readers becomes superfluous here. No child can be too young to learn the moral lesson of the piece: the necessity for the artist to preserve his or her freedom to create. The sweet and charming Princess September, mindful of manners and general etiquette, basks in the very innocence with which sensitive children (particularly the affluent among them) can easily relate. She cannot be comforted by her insensitive sisters upon the death of her parrot. Only the artistry of the nightingale can ease her sorrow—as well as her hunger, because her equally insensitive mother had sent her to bed without her dinner for being so overcome. His pastoral song relative to the landscape that she knows only too well delights her, and he will, eventually, sing her to sleep. Both the nightingale, as artist and performer, and September, as listener, prove most courteous to each another. Maugham, the dramatist, points quickly but emphatically, in the direction of theatrical propriety. He drives home the relationship between audience and performer, and the child reader learns still another lesson.

However, the most important lesson of all must be transmitted to the child reader: the meaning of freedom. As a child, September does not understand why the nightingale cannot share her notion of the advantages to be gained from captivity. After all, the bird resides in a golden cage made by the best workman in her father's kingdom. He will have three meals per day served by her maids of honor. He will not have a single care in the world, and thus he can sit in his cage and sing to his heart's content. She simply does not understand that while "all the world's a stage," the true artist cannot spend every moment of life locked inside of the theater.

At the end of the piece, Maugham, for the benefit of his reader, has reduced life to two simple but distinct stages: For almost the entire story, one has observed September as the child princess, anchored firmly but willingly to the captivity of childhood, and thus she does not really understand the meaning of freedom—artistic or spiritual. Then, at its very end, the writer reveals the effects of the nightingale's artistic and spiritual freedom upon the child. He unveils September as having grown into an extremely beautiful young woman; she marries the king of Cambodia and goes off to a new land on a white elephant. The dour Maugham, from his sickbed in a Bangkok hotel, makes a wish, and at that moment, autobiography and fantasy join hands.

W. SOMERSET MAUGHAM

W. Somerset Maugham (1874–1965) was an English novelist and playwright. With the success of his first novel, *Liza of Lambeth* (1897), he became committed to the writing life. His later novels include *Of Human Bondage* (1915), *The Moon and Sixpence* (1919), and *The Razor's Edge* (1944). In 1928, he settled in the south of France and from there pursued his travels around the world.

RICHARD C. JONES

Richard C. Jones (born in 1910) was an American illustrator who spent his early years in Chicago and Pennsylvania before moving to New York, where he worked as a book illustrator. In 1951, his work appeared in *Plantonio, the Pride of the Plain; A Ballad of the Old West.*

JAN MORRIS

Jan Morris is an acclaimed journalist and travel writer. Her many books include *The World of Venice, Journeys, Among the Cities, Manhattan '45, Hong Kong,* and most recently, *Fifty Years of Europe: An Album.* She lives in Wales.

SAMUEL J. ROGAL

Samuel J. Rogal is the the author of *A William Somerset Maugham Encyclopedia* and *A Companion to the Characters in the Fiction and Drama of W. Somerset Maugham.* He is chair of the Division of Humanities and Fine Arts at Illinois Valley Community College in Oglesby, Illinois.

THE IONA AND PETER OPIE LIBRARY OF CHILDREN'S LITERATURE

The Opie Library brings to a new generation an exceptional selection of children's literature, ranging from facsimiles and new editions of classic works to lost or forgotten treasures—some never before published—by eminent authors and illustrators. The series honors Iona and Peter Opie, the distinguished scholars and collectors of children's literature, continuing their lifelong mission to seek out and preserve the very best books for children.

ROBERT G. O'MEALLY, GENERAL EDITOR

Gold

Represents

Heaven:

How YOU Can Use COLORS
to Share the Gospel

Bob Dudley

DEDICATION

Dedicated to all my brothers and sisters in Christ who have walked with me around the world, sharing the gospel in love and patience.

CONTENTS

PRAFACE

When Cathy and I first graduated from seminary, we took a job as co-executive directors of Christian Farmers Outreach (CFO). We had actually worked a bit with CFO through our church while we were attending seminary. CFO would sponsor booths at local county farm fairs where they would use a rawhide bracelet with colored beads to give a gospel presentation to anyone who would stop to listen.

Eventually, Cathy and I would also work with Praise & Thunder (a ministry that served several different groups but concentrated on bikers). We introduced the salvation bracelets (what we called the rawhide bracelets) to bike blessings. It worked great.

Once Caty and I expanded to the biker community, we were unstoppable. We started using the salvation bracelets at carnivals, craft shows, state fairs, church block parties, bus ministries, short term mission trips, the list was only as small as our imaginations.

Eventually, Cathy and I broke from CFO and started

our own foundation (Lura B Walker Foundation). The main purpose of the foundation was to teach Christians how to share their faith and to teach pastors how to grow their church. To do this, we designed the Everyday Evangelism Program. This is a 12-step plan for sharing your faith. The main training took is a tract called "Do You Know?".

Thought the "Do You Know?" tract is meant to be used all by itself, it is also color coded to be used with the salvation bracelet or anything else you can come up with that has the salvation colors. Throughout this book, to keep life easy, I assume you are using the salvation bracelets and the "Do You Know" tract.

I would like to thank all the people that have helped me through the years…the hundreds of Christians that have manned booths and tents for me at state and county fairs, carnivals, craft shows and roadside tables. Also, all the brothers and sisters in Christ that have used our Salvation Bracelets on short-term mission trips and for their everyday evangelism needs. I have seen the bracelets used tens of thousands of times. This has helped me to refine the essence of using them in almost any witnessing situation.

I also want to thank Debbie Anderson, my editor AND sister-in-law. This book would not be possible without her. Thanks, sis.

INTRODUCTION

I first put the material together in this book when I would visit churches before a fair or short term mission trip. They would want training in how to use the salvation bracelets without going through a complete course in personal evangelism.

This book, then, is great for anyone or any church getting ready for an event where they need to witness but they are rusty or never have had the opportunity.

I have broken the book into several logical chapters.

Chapter 1 is just a short Bible study about why it is important for ALL Christians to share their faith.

Chapters 2, 3, 4 and 5 cover everything from getting into a spiritual conversation wherever you are to what to say for each color and how to actually lead someone to pray to accept Christ.

I added Chapter 6 for all of my brothers and sisters who have incorporated the color blue. When I first started using the salvation bracelets, we only had five colors. But, I have noticed more and more churches incorporating blue. And, funny enough, I have found three different ways they use blue. I've tried to do them all justice.

Chapter 7 deals with some items that really didn't fit anywhere else. I talk about how to deal with questions you may encounter. I also talk about the two most important questions you can ever ask another person. I also give a bit of emphasis on prayer.

Chapter 8 is complements of my wife, Cathy. I like to be given concepts and then figure out how I am going to make the process mine. Cathy, on the other hand, loves to have a script to follow. She asked me to write out a sample encounter for those of you like her – you work better if you have a script to follow. Since adding this section, I have had hundreds of people tell me it was one of the most important sections.

In Chapter 9, I listed a lot of the illustrations I use in my everyday witnessing. These illustrations work with the salvation bracelet AND they work with any other witnessing encounter you may have. Do you have any illustrations? Let others know by sharing on our Facebook group page – *Gold Represents Heaven.*

In chapter 10 I do one of my favorite things in the whole world – I tell the stories of people who have come to Christ. I want to encourage you to share the stories you become a part of. If you need a place to share these stories, please put these on our Facebook group page.

Chapter 11 is probably the most important chapter in the entire book. If you, personally, have never made a commitment to Christ, in this chapter I will show you how to do that.

My prayer is that you have as much of a blessing reading this book as I had writing it. The information in this book has helped thousands of Christians to share their faith in a simple and effective manner. Let me know if it works for you. God bless!

Bob Dudley

WHY DO WE DO WHAT WE DO?

A close friend of mine, Mike Khoury, is fond of saying:

Every Christian has two things in common with every other Christian. They are on their way to heaven and someone told them how to get there. Who are you going to tell?

Reading through the Bible, I have found over 20 different reasons to tell others about Jesus and what He is offering to the lost. I would like to talk about just two of those here.

Getting Close to God

There is a statistic out there that says only 5% of Christians have ever actually led someone to Christ. In other words, only a few of us have ever presented the gospel and led someone through the sinner's prayer.

I was saved when I was a teenager. Then I joined the army and never looked back. In the last 30 years I would be in the 95% of Christians that never led anyone to Christ — that was "someone else's job." It wasn't until 2004 that I listened to God and realized that it wasn't someone else's job — it was MY job! Once I

1

learned a plan and was taught that we're not alone — God works with us — it became much easier to witness.   *- Bob Dudley*

How would you like to personally be responsible for upping that percentage of Christians that have led someone to Christ? The next time your church has an outreach event, see if you can share the gospel using the colors. Maybe, you can even use the salvation bracelets we will talk about later.

When you want to get close to your dad you find out what he is interested in and you develop an interest in that, also. If your dad is interested in fishing you ask him to take you with him and to teach you how to fish.

I remember when my mother married my step-father. I was about 12 years old. He loved me like a son. I wanted to get close to him. I was too young to know why I did what I did. But, I found out what he was interested in and I became interested in that, also. He loved to go fishing. When he wasn't fishing he would spend the weekends working on his fishing gear in the garage. I would find myself going in there, asking him questions about fishing and what he was doing and trying to get interested in what he was doing. For me to get close to his heart I became interested in what was already close to his heart.

It's the same with God. If you want to be close to God, our heavenly Father, then you need to find out what is close to His heart and get it close to your heart. God is interested in saving the lost.

There really isn't anything that God would rather do than see lost sinners come to a saving knowledge of His Son, Jesus Christ.

For the Son of man is come to seek and to save that which was lost. (Luke 19:10)

If you are a parent you may know the fear of having a child lost in a store or at the playground. To say the least, it is not a comfortable feeling. Just imagining of what might happen to your child is frightening. God *knows* what will happen to those people that remain lost for eternity. How much more does He want to see everyone saved?

It's good to work in Sunday School or the choir, or any of a dozen other ministries. God needs workers everywhere you look. But, if you want there to be joy in heaven, if you want the angels to sing – lead one lost sinner to Christ.

I say unto you, that likewise joy shall be in heaven over one sinner that repenteth, more than over ninety and nine just persons, which need no repentance. (Luke 15:7)

Likewise, I say unto you, there is joy in the presence of the angels of God over one sinner that repenteth. (Luke 15:10)

Always remember, as much as you might want to see someone saved, God wants it more. It is His will that none should perish.

The Lord is not slack concerning his promise, as some men count slackness; but is longsuffering to us-ward, not willing that any should perish, but that all should come to repentance. (2 Peter 3:9)

For God so loved the world, that he gave his only begotten Son, that whosoever believeth in him should not perish, but have everlasting life. (John 3:16)

Working WITH God

Some of you might be thinking that you don't know how to witness, that you are afraid, that it's not for you and you just can't do it.

When you go with your dad to fish the first time, he doesn't leave you there to fend for yourself. He helps you bait the hook and throw in the line. He may even help you reel in your first catch.

When you go out to fish for men, God does not send you out alone, either. In the great commission recorded in Matthew's gospel, Christ promises to be with you whenever you go out to talk to others about Him, even unto the end of the world. When you talk to someone about Jesus, He is standing there right next to you.

and, lo, I am with you alway, even unto the end of the world. (Matthew 28:20b)

Not only is Jesus there with you, God also promises to give you the power of the Holy Spirit. Pastor Don Frazier says, "If you want to feel the presence of the Holy Spirit so close the hairs on the back of your neck stand up, tell someone what Jesus did for them and how they can get to heaven."

But ye shall receive power, after that the Holy Ghost is come upon you: and ye shall be witnesses unto me. (Acts 1:8a)

And, as if THAT wasn't enough, you have the supernatural power of God's Holy Scriptures.

So then faith cometh by hearing, and hearing by the word of God. (Romans 10:17)

And, to top it all off, the Holy Spirit is working on the heart of the person you are talking to:

And when he is come, he will reprove the world of sin, and of righteousness, and of judgment: (John 16:8)

Never forget, you are the junior partner of the most awesome team ever assembled in the history of the universe. Everyone on the team has a job. It is not your job to convince, just to convey. It is the job of God to convince.

God Will Save Anyone, If You Will Let Him

On Saturday I was talking to a young lady that had never been married and had four children. She had had her first child when she was just 14. As I talked to her and shared the gospel she told me that God could never forgive her and that she just couldn't believe that Jesus died for her sins. Nothing I said would change her mind. Finally, I told her that she should think about it and, if she changed her mind, to come back and I would show her how to invite Jesus to be her Savior.

Monday night, as we were packing up around 10 PM, we were talking about a man that had just walked away from the booth without accepting Christ. One of the workers in the booth was saying that we never know when God's word will bear fruit. Just as she said that, I looked to the table in the front of the booth and the girl from Saturday was standing there. I went up and asked her how she was doing. She just said, "I'm ready." I held her hands and we bowed our heads as she asked Jesus to save her.

Soul Winning and Everyday Evangelism

This is a testimony from Cathy Dudley

Before my world was turned upside down by *Everyday Evangelism*, I was a good Christian, so I thought. For ten years I drove a needy child to church, people praised me and I basked in the praises. But, in hindsight, it was a sad testimony. In those ten years I never once shared the gospel.

The beginning of my adventure was when my husband, Bob, came to me with this foolish idea to witness. I said, "Um, ok, I can support you but I would never be able to talk to anyone." I was wrong about that, for God had other plans.

I went with Bob to the *Everyday Evangelism* International Directors' College and, after Thursday evening visitation, I got so excited because the plan was so simple, I said to my husband, "I think I can visit someone in their home if they visited the church first." I took one baby step toward God's will.

The last night of the directors' college, Jim (one of the church members) said, "You ride the DC metro. Wow! You can witness to two people a day."

When Jim was out of earshot, I said to my husband, "He is plum crazy and there is no way on this earth that I will ever witness on the metro." I was wrong about that for God had other plans.

Next it was time for me to be a trainer. My husband suggested the idea and I gave him a three-day tantrum of why this was totally impossible. But I was wrong about that and God had other plans. I was so adamant about this one that I challenged God to show me that I could be a trainer. Needless to say, God won that challenge.

I want you to know that in God's power: I have witnessed to people on bus visitation, on the street, on the metro (thanks, Jim), in the home and trained several others to witness. I do not know of anyone who has fought the Lord more along the way than I have. I tell people, "If you have not taken the *Everyday Evangelism*, please stop fighting the Lord's will. I've done enough fighting for both of us."

You remember that little girl that I drove to church for 10 years? She is not so little anymore. Bob and I went back to Ohio to visit her and had the chance to lead her to the Lord. Imagine my pain if I had not had a second change. Ten years driving her around showing love but no salvation. But we only needed five minutes, once we had a plan. And now Nicky is on her way to heaven. *Everyday*

Evangelism did turn my world upside down - in a way that I would never undo.

GETTING STARTED

Pray before, during and after you witness. God listens to the prayers of the soul winner. We'll discuss God's answers to prayers later. But, for now, whenever you are looking to share the gospel – pray that God will work in the lives of the people you will be talking with.

No matter where you find yourself witnessing (everyday encounters, short-term mission trips or working at a fair) try to keep it short. Peter was able to lead the entire household of Cornelius to the Lord in under 2 minutes. Time yourself reading the passage, below:

34 Then Peter opened his mouth, and said, Of a truth I perceive that God is no respecter of persons: 35 But in every nation he that feareth him, and worketh righteousness, is accepted with him. 36 The word which God sent unto the children of Israel, preaching peace by Jesus Christ: (he is Lord of all:) 37 That word, I say, ye know, which was published throughout all Judaea, and began from Galilee, after the baptism which John preached; 38 How God anointed Jesus of Nazareth with the Holy Ghost and with power: who went about doing good, and healing all that were oppressed of the devil; for God was with him. 39 And we are witnesses of all *things which he did both in the land of the Jews, and in Jerusalem; whom they slew and hanged on a tree: *[40]* Him God raised up the third day, and shewed him openly; *[41]* Not to all the people, but unto witnesses chosen before of God, even to us, who did eat and drink with him after he rose from the dead. *[42]* And he commanded us to preach unto the people, and to testify that it is he which was ordained of God to be the Judge of quick and dead. *[43]* To him give all the prophets witness, that through his name whosoever believeth in him shall receive remission of sins. (Acts 10:34-43)*

Everyday Encounters

In my everyday witnessing I use the plan taught in *Everyday Evangelism*. This is a very effective method of witnessing and is, actually, the plan that I first learned and what the *Do You Know?* tract is based on.

But I still try to keep a few Salvation Bracelets on hand. I find they are very good to use in situations where the person you are led to deal with is in a hurry or has a short attention span. This may be children, service personnel (maid, doorman, waiter or waitress, to name a few) or senior citizens.

Being Friendly

As with every witnessing opportunity, the first step is to be interested in them as a person. Be folksy. Get to know something about them – their name, where they work, where they go to church. Everyone is lonely. Everyone wants a friend.

Can I Give You a Gift?

After I have chatted with the person I want to witness to, I usually ask them if I can give them a small gift – a bracelet. I then ask if they have ever seen the colors put together this way. Whether they have or not, I will ask their permission to share their meaning with them.

Short-Term Mission Trip

A great way to use the Salvation Bracelets is on short term mission trips. The bracelets have been used to lead thousands to Christ around the world. Here I will talk about two ways they are used. But, let your imagination run wild.

Wear Them Yourself

Whatever your mission, you can use the Salvation Bracelets to bring the message home. If you wear the bracelet while on your trip, eventually someone will ask you about it. And, if they don't, as you are finishing up whatever you are doing with them, you can offer one as a gift. This is a very easy and very non-threatening way to get the gospel to someone as you show them the love of Jesus through your actions. Remember, faith comes by *hearing* not by *watching*.

Use Them to Pass the Time

A good friend of mine, Wayne, went on a short-term dental hygiene mission trip. Wayne was in charge of keeping the people occupied while they stood in line to see the dentist. Wayne would have groups of four or five sit in front of him as the line moved into the building. They would hear the gospel message, he would give them an opportunity to accept Christ, then they would proceed down the line to the dentist. He led hundreds of souls to Christ that way.

Talking to the Maid

The maid came to clean my room, so I had to do a walkabout. I went out to the beach and started talking to the staff. The life guard and the maintenance man were both saved. We had a great conversation. After we talked awhile I headed from the beach back to the hotel.

I had to pass the outdoor bar area. I happened to be wearing a shirt with CIA in big letters and "Confidence in the Almighty" in small lettering right underneath it. As I passed the bar one of the bartenders asked me if I worked for the CIA. An opening.

I walked over to them and started a conversation – no one else was around. I steered it to the spiritual and found out that the male bartender grew up Baptist but didn't go to church now. The female bartender was Seventh Day Adventist. Within a few minutes they bowed their heads together, right there at the bar with the drinks behind them and the reggae music all around them. They asked Jesus to be their Savior. They said they would come to the church service the next Sunday.

Working at a Fair

The Booth Captain or a greeter will invite people into the booth to receive a free gift with a message. The gift can be any number of things – a simple beaded bracelet, tote bag, bandana, walking stick – this is limited only by the imagination. When they bring the people (could be one or a few) to sit in front of you, there are a couple of things you can do to set the mood before you give the message of the beads.

How's the Fair? (Being Friendly)

The first thing you want to do is get them comfortable and talking. You can ask them about the fair, or about a hat or shirt logo they are wearing. As you are talking, hand them a tract to keep. Basically, be your normal, caring self – be a Christian.

Who We Are (a Christian Outreach Ministry)

To get on the topic of spiritual matters, it's good to point to the sign and tell them that you are with a Christian Outreach Ministry and you are giving the gospel message with a free gift. You may ask them if they have a church that they attend regularly. Most people will be very responsive to this since they know you represent a Christian organization.

Alabama Sports Show

Marcus (one of my soul-winning partners) and I were in Alabama working in a booth handing out free walking sticks with a gospel message. While there, we became good friends with Roger. Roger was there selling his wares. But, in his spare time he had an evangelism ministry so he was pretty interested in what we were doing.

On the second day Roger came over during his break, hoping to watch Marcus present the gospel a few times — maybe pick up a pointer or two. While he was standing in the aisle waiting for Marcus to finish with a group of teenagers he felt a tap on his shoulder. It was Steve, an old high school buddy he hadn't seen in 20 years.

Roger asked him what he was doing there. Steve said he had been walking around the show and saw several people carrying walking sticks. He heard he could get one at this booth and wondered what he had to do to get one. Roger, recalling that he and his friends had witnessed to Steve for years in school in vain said, "All you have to do is listen to that guy for a few minutes and you get the stick for free."

Steve said, "I can do that." After the teenagers left Roger and Steve sat down in front of Marcus. Marcus asked Steve, "Are you 100% sure, if you were to die today, that you would go to heaven?" Steve wasn't sure and Marcus had the opportunity to show him, through accepting Jesus as his Savior, he could be sure. Steve bowed his head and asked Jesus to come into his heart.

Roger spent the rest of the day calling all his friends and telling them about the harvest he had seen that day from a seed they had planted 20 years ago. Never, never give up on your friends and loved ones – you never know when they will finally see the light.

Everyday Evangelism and The Message of the Beads

Everyday Evangelism was created in November 2013 when Cathy and I decided to expand our reach beyond *Agora Evangelism* (our first ministry). The two of us were brainstorming on a ministry that would have a two-fold mission:

- Reach as many people as possible in the world with the gospel of Jesus Christ.

- Develop a fast and effective method for teaching Christians to share their faith in all situations.

We came up with *Everyday Evangelism*. It would combine the ease and effectiveness of the gospel presentation taught in *The Four Spiritual Laws*, *Evangelism Explosion*, *Operation Go* and *Soul Winners' Club* with the visual cues of the colors used by Charles Spurgeon and made famous in the wordless book by *Child Evangelism Fellowship*.

In the last seven years, Cathy and I have had the privilege of giving out over 125,000 gospel presentations, and have been instrumental in leading over 32,000 people to Christ and have trained over 1,000 Christians to share their faith in an easy and effective way.

Everyday Evangelism has been a blessing to thousands of people around the world. By using the colors of the beads (gold, black, red, white and green), anyone can give the gospel in an easy-to-understand format.

My prayer is that you will give *Everyday Evangelism* a chance, that you will give God a chance, to work through you. If you do this, you will see miracles that you never thought possible. You will see lives transformed through the renewing power of the gospel of Jesus Christ.

THE MESSAGE OF THE BEADS

The best thing about the *Message of the Beads* ministry is you don't have to be an experienced soul winner to do it. As a matter of fact, it's perfect for the Christian that has never had an opportunity to share their faith with anyone. Many people have been saved in this ministry by simply having a Christian read the tract to them while they looked at the beads. Remember, it is your job to convey the gospel and it's God's job to convince the sinner to come to Christ.

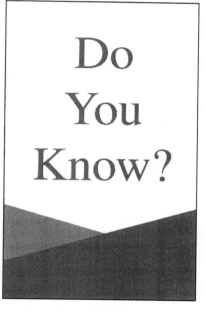

In this section we will present the gospel as it is outlined with the beads. All you have to do is be willing to tell the gospel. The Scriptures are supernatural and able to convict the hearts of those that will listen.

So then faith cometh by hearing, and hearing by the word of God. (Romans 10:17)

For the word of God is quick, and powerful, and sharper than any two edged sword, piercing even to the dividing asunder of soul and spirit, and of the joints and marrow, and is a discerner of the thoughts and intents of the heart. (Hebrews 4:12)

Even if you read the gospel from the tract, this will be a clear presentation of the gospel. And it may be the only clear presentation they ever receive. Take your time and listen to the leading of the Holy Spirit. Never forget, our ministry is sharing the Gospel not giving out free trinkets.

GOLD: Eternal Life in Heaven

> ### Heaven
>
> **Somewhere we all want to go.**
>
> *"...and the city was pure gold like unto clear glass." Revelation 21:18b*
>
> **What if your life were to end today? Are you 100% certain you would go to Heaven?**

As the tract says, the gold bead represents heaven. Spend a minute or two talking about heaven and what it is like. Talk about its perfection and the fact that gold represents this perfection. Towards the end of this book are some useful illustrations to use for the different parts of the gospel. Feel free to do your best to explain this and all other parts of the gospel. I'll even tell them that I hope to go to heaven one day.

But, What if They Don't Believe in Heaven?

I'm often asked in training sessions: what if they don't believe in … (heaven, the Bible, God)? This is a very good question and one that is easy to answer from a biblical perspective.

The thing to remember is that it doesn't matter (at first) what they believe. The Bible tells us that "faith comes by hearing and hearing by the word of God." (Romans 10:17) If you can get someone to listen to you, then you have a chance for the Holy Spirit to use His word, the Bible, to speak to their heart.

I recall once having a mother and her son (he was in his twenties) come into our booth. The mother was saved and knew what we were doing. Her son was a professed atheist. He wanted nothing to do with God and sat down to appease his mother and to get a free gift. As I went through the gospel it was interesting (almost comical) to watch the change come over him.

As I talked about sin and Romans 3:23 his eyes were all over the place looking around. He was watching everything and everyone but me.

As I talked about the wages of sin and Romans 6:23 his eyes played around my head but never actually looking directly at me.

As I talked about Jesus dying on the cross for us and Romans 5:8 he started looking at me but not, yet, looking me in the eye.

Finally, as I spoke about our response to what Jesus did for us and Romans 10:13 he was looking directly at me. He was completely focused on what I had to say and what the Bible had to say.

As his mother looked on, tears rolling down her cheeks, he bowed his head and asked Jesus to forgive him and be his Savior.

When you engage someone to talk to them about the gospel, it doesn't matter what they believe. All that matters is that they are willing to listen to God's word. If they are willing to do that, then God can convict their hearts and save their souls.

The "Question" (Getting on the Subject)

After you talk about heaven then it's time to get down to business. It's handy to know their spiritual state, as best you can, before you present the gospel. A very good, non-threatening, way to do that is with the "question." You can ask them something like this:

If someone was to ask you, "Are you 100% sure, if you were to die today, that you would go to heaven?" — what would you tell them?

You will get several different answers to this. If they say anything except, "Yes, I've trusted Jesus Christ alone to get me to heaven" (or something similar) then chances are they are not saved. If they say "yes" with no qualifiers, then you can ask the follow-up question:

Can I ask you, if you were standing at the gates of heaven and Jesus asked you why He should let you in, what would you tell Him?

Again, keep your spiritual antenna up. Begin with the Spirit's help to discern which of the people in front of you are saved and which ones are lost. Jesus said He would help you here.

The "Question"

It is always important, before witnessing to someone, that you first determine their spiritual state. I recall witnessing to a group of five teenage boys (all around 17 or 18 years old) at a fair one year.

They came into the booth we had set up. They were all happy and joking. They were good friends and were having fun at the fair. I asked them the question: "Are you boys 100% sure, if you died today, that you would go to heaven?" I had them answer one at a time.

The first boy told me how he had trusted Christ as his Savior when he was 12. The next one gave me a similar story. The third one, also, knew when he had trusted Jesus. The fourth one told me he was sure about heaven because he was a good boy and went to church. The fifth one told about asking Jesus to be his Savior.

All of a sudden the joking stopped as four of the boys realized, for the first time, that their friend would not spend an eternity in heaven with them. He was trusting in his good works and not in the blood of Jesus.

I knew instantly who to focus on. Asking the "question" was priceless. I ignored the four boys and just talked to the one. I went through the colored beads with him and told him the message of Jesus. In a matter of minutes he bowed his head and asked Jesus to be his Savior, just like all his friends had already done.

Walking away from the booth, the merriment resumed as the four boys welcomed their friend, now their brother, into the family.

BLACK: Sin

Sin & Its Penalty

You have sinned against God.

"For all have sinned, and come short of the glory of God." Romans 3:23

There is a penalty for sin.

"For the wages of sin is death." Romans 6:23.

Here is the first piece of bad news. We are all sinners. From the time we are born until the time we die we have a sin nature inherited from our parents.

Jesus tells us in the Great Commission to teach. Teach them here that they have sinned against God.

Because of our sin we cannot enter into God's perfect heaven. Rather, if we are paid (our wages) what we are owed for our sins, we are destined for an eternity in hell where we can never, ever get out. There is nothing we can do, once we fall short of God's glory we are forever separated from Him. Unless He does something to bridge the gap.

The Ministry of the Holy Spirit to the Lost

The ministry of the Holy Spirit to the lost is given in John 16:8.

And when he is come, he will reprove the world of sin, and of righteousness, and of judgment:

The Holy Spirit does this through the Word of God — the Bible. Hebrews 4:12.

For the word of God is quick, and powerful, and sharper than any two edged sword, piercing even to the dividing asunder of soul and spirit, and of the joints and marrow, and is a discerner of the thoughts and intents of the heart.

If you talk to enough people, you will see this in action. I was working at an evangelism tent at a craft fair in West Virginia. A man stepped into our tent to get a walking stick with a message. He was in his mid to late 30's.

I showed him the beads. After talking about the gold bead and heaven, I asked him if he was 100% sure he was going to heaven. He told me that he wasn't sure at all. "As a matter of fact," he said, "I am pretty sure I am not going to heaven."

I went to the black bead and quoted Romans 3:23.

For all have sinned and come short of the glory of God.

As I finished the verse, he broke down in tears of anguish. He just started crying right in front of me and everyone in the tent.

He asked me how I knew about his sins. He said, "How do you know what horrible things I've done? I've never met you."

Of course, I didn't know anything about what he had done. But God knew and God convicted his heart through God's word.

RED: *Christs Blood*

Now for the good news. Two thousand years ago God the Son came down from heaven, took on the form of

> ## The Blood of Christ
>
> Jesus died on the cross, was buried and rose again, victorious over sin, Hell and the grave.
>
> *"But God commendeth his love toward us, in that, while we were yet sinners, Christ died for us." Romans 5:8*

man, lived a perfect life for 33 years, died on the cross for our sins and (on the third day) rose from the dead.

Talk of Christ's perfection. Because of His perfection, He was able to take the wages for our sins.

God knew we couldn't get to heaven on our own so He gave us a way – a free gift through Jesus Christ. All we have to do is be willing to trust completely what Christ did on the cross to pay for our sins. We can't pay for it, we can't work for it – all we can do is accept it. And that brings us to the white bead.

WHITE: *Our Response*

Jesus is able and willing to save you from your sin penalty.

"For whosoever shall call upon the name of the Lord shall be saved." Romans 10:13

Even though Jesus died on the cross for everyone's sins, not everyone goes to heaven.

We need to see our need for forgiveness and realize that Jesus cared enough to pay for that forgiveness. We have to believe. This means trust in Jesus fully. We have to make a conscious decision to trust Jesus as our only way to heaven.

There must be a moment in our lives where we personally decide that:

- Jesus died for our sins,
- Jesus rose from the dead, and
- We are going to trust Him completely as our only way to heaven.

Once we ask Jesus to come into our heart and save us, we are washed as white as snow.

Now is the time that you should ask them to pray to receive Christ as their Savior. But, before you move to the prayer, you might want to spend a minute reviewing what you have talked about and see if they are in agreement with you. Ask them:

- *Do you believe that you are a sinner?*
- *Do you believe, like the Bible says, that there is a penalty for our sins?*
- *Do you believe that, 2000 years ago, God sent His Son to earth to die for our sins and then, three days later, He Jesus rose from the dead?*

Bob Dudley

PRAYER

John R. Rice said prayer is asking God what we need. Prayer is how we communicate to God. In a sermon on prayer, Billy Sunday said:

- Elijah prayed and God answered with fire.
- Hannah prayed and Samuel was born.
- Daniel prayed and the lions were muzzled.
- The apostles prayed and the Holy Spirit came down.
- Luther prayed and the Reformation was the result.
- Knox prayed and Scotland trembled.
- Wesley prayed and millions were moved Godward.
- Whitefield prayed and thousands were converted.
- Finney prayed and mighty revivals resulted.
- Taylor prayed and the great China Inland Mission was born.
- Muller prayed and over $7 million was sent in to feed 1,000s of orphans.
- Auntie Cook prayed and Moody was anointed.
- Men are always praying, God is always answering.

We are going to pray three times here. First, we are going to pray that the Holy Spirit will convict their hearts. Then, hopefully, we will pray with them to ask Jesus to come into their hearts. Finally, we will pray thanks to God that they got saved.

Prayer Works

I had gone out on visitation to check on someone that had trusted Christ as their Savior the previous week. After we had spent a bit of time giving her reassurance of her salvation, we decided to knock on some doors. As we were walking down the way a man jogged across the street towards us and engaged us in conversation.

He asked, "What church are you guys from?"

"What makes you think we're from a church?"

"You're wearing suits on a Saturday morning. You're either cops or Christians. I figured I'd go for Christians."

We traded pleasantries for a time. It turns out his wife and adult children were all saved. He, on the other hand, was a Jehovah's Witness. As a matter of fact, when his family came out to see who he was talking with, one of his sons had a shirt with the Romans Road (Rom 3:23; 6:23; 5:8; 10:13) printed on the front.

He allowed me to share the gospel with him. He related that he had heard it numerous times from his family. As soon as I explained Romans 10:13 to him, I asked him if he would like to trust Jesus as his only way to heaven. He said, "No."

We talked for a little and I asked him again. Again, he said, "No."

After a bit, I tried a third time. Still, "No."

Then it hit me. I forgot to pray that God would convict his heart. I told him we had to go soon. I then asked if it would be OK for me to pray for him before we left.

"Sure," he said.

I prayed out loud, "Dear Father, thank you for Tom's honesty – that he isn't sure if he died, he would go to heaven. Would you speak to his heart and show him that Jesus is your Son, is God? Would you convict his heart and let him know he needs your Son?"

I then asked him one more time, with confidence, "If Jesus is willing to accept you just the way you are, and He is, would you be willing to accept Him and trust Him as your only way to heaven?"

He said, "Yes."

I turned to his son with the Romans Road t-shirt and asked him if he would like to lead his father in the sinner's pray. With tears all around, his wife and three sons circling him, he prayed to ask Jesus to come into his heart.

Pray That They Will be Saved

There are several verses in the Bible that promise an answer to the prayer of a Christian. In particular, the following verses promise that if we pray in His will He will hear us and answer our prayers.

If ye abide in me, and my words abide in you, ye shall ask what ye will, and it shall be done unto you. Herein is my Father glorified, that ye bear much fruit; so shall ye be my disciples. (John 15:7-8)

And this is the confidence that we have in him, that, if we ask any thing according to his will, he heareth us: And if we know that he hear us, whatsoever we ask, we know that we have the petitions that we desired of him. (1 John 5:14-15)

What could be more in God's will than someone accepting Christ as their Savior?

The Lord is not slack concerning his promise, as some men count slackness; but is longsuffering to us-ward, not willing that any should perish, but that all should come to repentance. (2 Peter 3:9)

So, it is very profitable to pray for exactly what you want before you ask the person in front of you if they would like to receive Christ as their Savior. Also, it is a good idea to pray for this out loud. This lets the person, or people, in front of you know that it is OK to pray out loud in public.

Ask the person, or persons, if you can pray for them and then bow your head and ask God (aloud) for exactly what you want. Pray something like this:

(First ask) *May I pray for us?*

(Then bow your head) *Dear God, thank You for bringing us together and thank You for Mr. Jones' willingness to listen to Your word and for his honesty in telling me that he is not sure he is on his way to heaven. I pray now that You will speak to his heart about his need for Jesus as his Savior.*

Do not say "Amen." You want to keep them in an attitude of prayer when you ask them the next question.

Pray With Them to Get Saved

> If the Lord Jesus is willing to receive you just the way you are, and He is, would you be willing to receive Him and ask Him to come into your heart and save you?
>
> If you will, then, right now (in simple faith) pray this prayer, asking the Lord to forgive you of your sin and save you:
>
> "Dear Lord, I know that I am a sinner, I know that Jesus died on the cross for me. Please forgive me of my sin, come into my heart, and save me. In Jesus' name, Amen."
>
> God Bless You! Today you have made the most important decision in your life. Jesus is your Savior, your sin is forgiven and you have a home in Heaven.
>
> – Bob Dudley

As soon as you finish your prayer, a good question to ask them is:

I have just one more question, if Jesus is willing to accept you just the way you are, and He is, would you be willing to trust Him as your only way to heaven?

There are a lot of ways to ask someone to accept Christ. The question, above, is found to be a very gentle and very positive way to invite someone into God's family. Whatever question you use, make sure you are helping the Holy Spirit and not hindering. You might be asking yourself, "How do I hinder the Holy Spirit?" If you invite someone into the kingdom by saying, "You don't want to get saved, do you?" or "Haven't you done that before, everyone has done that?" you might be hindering.

It is best, if you don't have a lot of experience here, to just memorize (or read from the tract) the question we suggest here.

If they say, "Yes," (they want to accept Jesus as their

only way to heaven) then explain to them that you are going to lead them in a phrase-by-phrase prayer. Make sure they understand the prayer is not a magic chant. Salvation is based on what they believe in their heart. You are just helping them to tell God what they believe and have accepted. The prayer can be something like this:

Dear Jesus,
I know that I am a sinner.
I know You died on the cross for me.
Please forgive me of my sin,
come into my heart and save me.
In Jesus' name, Amen.

It is perfectly acceptable to read the prayer on *The Message* tract that you have given them.

Pray Thanks That They Were Saved

A good thing to do after someone accepts Christ and goes from an eternity in hell to eternal life with God is to pray a prayer of thanksgiving with them. You can do this right away or just before they leave the booth.

When you have finished praying with them, show them the **Birth Certificate** side of the tract and have them sign and date it. Today is their spiritual birthday! Once they sign and date the certificate, have them read it back to you.

ASSURANCE AND GROWTH

Trusting Christ is just the start of the journey. Each person that prays to receive Christ at your event is a new babe in Christ and it would be good if we could give him a little help to go in the right direction.

I Thought I had Lost My Salvation

The two ladies had walked up to our booth at the county fair, hand in hand. After a few minutes of small talk I asked them both if they were 100% sure about going to heaven. One girl said, with a slight smile on her face, she was sure she would not go. The other girl said, sheepishly, "At one time I thought I was, but I don't think so any more."

I asked the second girl to hold that thought while I dealt with the first. After I talked about sin, I asked the first girl if she had ever sinned in her life. She said, "Yes, we are lesbians and we live together." I asked the two of them if they thought that was a sin. Both of them, together, said, "Yes, of course it's a sin."

Within a few minutes I led the first girl to a saving knowledge of Christ. I then turned to the second girl and asked her why she had thought at one time that she would go to heaven.

She told me, "When I was a young teen I asked Jesus to forgive me of my sins and to come into my heart to be my Savior."

I then asked her why she feels, now, that she would not go to heaven. She told me her pastor told her she could not be saved and live in the lifestyle she was living. He told her that there was no way she could be saved.

I showed her John 3:16 – For God so loved the world, that he gave his only begotten Son, that whosoever believeth in him should not perish, but have everlasting life.

I then asked her if she believed. She said, with a little hesitation in her voice, "Yes."

I then showed her Romans 10:9 – That if thou shalt confess with thy mouth the Lord Jesus, and shalt believe in thine heart that God hath raised him from the dead, thou shalt be saved.

I then asked her if she believed what it said.

She started crying and said, "Yes."

I then asked her if she were to die today, would she go to heaven.

Now the tears flowed freely down her face as, through trembling lips, she said, "Yes."

They both knew they had a sin problem. And now that they were both saved, they were willing to give it to God and work on it.

But, more importantly, they both understood that they were on their way to heaven, through the blood of Jesus, and no one could ever take that away from them.

Assurance of salvation is vital to Christian growth.

Assurance

The next most important thing to being saved is knowing that you are saved. Go back to the white bead and talk to the new Christian sitting in front of you about Romans 10:13. Show him that he is part of *whosoever*, that he

He Hideth My Soul

A wonderful Savior is Jesus, my Lord,
A wonderful Savior to me;
He hideth my soul in the cleft of the rock,
Where rivers of pleasure I see.

He hideth my soul in the cleft of the rock
That shadows a dry, thirsty land;
He hideth my life in the depths of His love,
And covers me there with His hand,
And covers me there with His hand.

called on the Lord (in prayer) and that **he IS saved**. Ask him where saved people go when they die. Emphasize that he is going to heaven.

Show him that he is saved forever. He is part of God's family and no one can take that away from him. Some useful verses (if you don't want to use Romans 10:13) are John 1:12 and John 3:16.

Keep in mind that this may be the last time you will talk to this new babe in Christ.

When you are sure they are secure in what they just did, then continue on with the green bead.

Who's Your Daddy?

When I was about 8-years-old, my parents got into a vicious argument. I was so scared that I ran to my dad and wrapped my little arms around his leg. As I stood there crying, my mom said to me, "I don't know why you went running to him. He's not your father."

That was how I learned that my mom had been married before and that she had divorced and remarried before I was 2 years old. Needless to say, my world was shattered. I had lost the assurance of knowing who my father was.

Growth

1. **Make a public profession of your faith this Sunday in church.** *"Whosoever therefore shall confess me before men, him will I confess also before my Father which is in heaven." Matthew 10:32*

2. **Follow the Lord in Baptism.** *"Then they that gladly received his word were baptized: and the same day there were added unto them about three thousand souls." Acts 2:41*

3. **Read your Bible daily.** *"Thy word is a lamp unto my feet, and a light unto my path." Psalm 119:105*

4. **Pray everyday.** *"The effectual fervent prayer of a righteous man availeth much." James 5:16*

5. **Attend a Bible-believing church regularly.** *"I was glad when they said unto me, Let us go into the house of the Lord." Psalm 122:1*

6. **Tell others about what Jesus did for you.** *"Go home to thy friends, and tell them how great things the Lord hath done for thee, and hath had compassion on thee." Mark 5:19*

7. **Give to God's work.** *"Give, and it shall be given unto you." Luke 6:38*

8. **Confess to God when you sin.** *"If we confess our sins, he is faithful and just to forgive us our sins, and to cleanse us from all unrighteousness." 1 John 1:9*

Make sure the new converts in front of you have no doubts in their minds that God is their heavenly Father and He will always be their Father. No one can ever take them out of God's family.

GREEN: Christian Growth

Don't leave him as a newborn baby with no guidance or way to grow. Remember, Jesus commanded us to save *and* disciple the lost.

Explain to him that he is saved and a child of God forever. But, if he wants to be an obedient child, there are certain things that God would want him to do. For instance, he needs to go to a good, Bible-believing church every week. He needs to pray and read his Bible every day. Quickly go over the back of the tract.

If your church is close, invite him to the next service. He probably will not understand the significance of what has happened to him by asking Jesus into his heart. His body is now the temple of the Holy Spirit (I Cor 6:19) and he is a child of the King (John 1:12). Over the next few days, among other things, he will have a more sensitive awareness of his own sinful nature. Without a proper grounding and nurturing it will be easy for him to misunderstand these changes inside him. He needs to be around others who can guide him properly.

Follow-Up is Critical

The young man, Johnny, visited our booth at a county fair. After watching two of his friends get saved, he came back the next night to talk with me. Johnny told me he was saved when he was 12 (he was now 14-years-old). He also told me he felt guilty ever since he walked into our booth yesterday. After some probing questions I found that he wasn't living for God.

I told him to go home and make an honest list of all the things he thought he had done wrong. I told him to individually confess and apologize for each of them. After he was finished, I told him to destroy the list. I told him to come back the next day to let me know what happened.

He came back in the morning. I asked how it went. He

told me that he cried. I asked how he felt now. He said he never felt better. This was 5 years ago. Next month I will be having lunch with Johnny. He is in college now and still living for God.

Follow-up and discipleship *cannot* be over emphasized.

Follow-Up Book

Give him a book to take home with him. Even if you invite him to church, the world may get in the way of this new babe in Christ. Make sure, before he leaves the booth, that he has a follow-up book in his hands.

Any follow-up or discipleship book that your church uses is fine. If you don't have one that you are currently using or would like to try a new one, AEM offers *Christian Growth*. It is an eight lesson booklet for Christian growth based on the eight steps on *The Message* tract and the *Soul Winners Club* tract.

Some Spanish tracts and follow up books may also be a good thing to keep handy.

Follow-Up Cards

When you give your new babe in Christ the follow-up book, you should also try to get their address so that your pastor, your church or (even) you can follow up with him.

At a minimum, you want to make sure he gets a letter of encouragement from your church. As a matter of fact, a good way to get their address is to simply say:

Do you mind if I have my pastor send you a letter of encouragement about what you did today or, possibly, have him visit you?

About half of the people, or more, will say "Yes." If they do, then hand them the ACS card (*I Have*

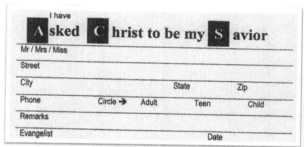

Asked Christ to be my Savior) and a pen. You may ask a child to get their parent's permission first and then you fill out the card as they give you the address. If they are from out of town, your church may try to get the person to a Bible-believing church near them.

Bob Dudley

WHAT ABOUT BLUE?

When I first started working with the Salvation Bracelets and using colors to present the gospel, I only knew about five colors: *gold, black, red, white,* and *green.* This was probably back around 2005. However, in the last few years I have been working with several churches who like having *blue* in the mix. The interesting thing is, they all have different meanings for blue. What I would like to do in this chapter is introduce some of the more common uses for *blue* and show you how to integrate them into the rest of the colors.

I've seen three primary uses for *blue*: faith, water baptism, baptism of the Holy Spirit. The first use of *blue,* faith, works well between the *red* and *white* colors. Both of the baptism uses seem to work best for me between the *white* and the *green* colors. So, let's look at how we can use blue to lead people to Christ and, perhaps, help them grow in Christ.

Blue Represents Faith
The verse Christians usually use when blue represents faith is Galatians 2:16.

Knowing that a man is not justified by the works of the law, but by the faith of Jesus Christ, even we have believed in Jesus Christ, that we might be justified by the faith of Christ, and not by the works of the law: for by the works of the law shall no flesh be justified.

Here is how I would integrate blue when it represents faith.

RED: I would talk about red as laid out in the book. I would end up with a description of the crucifixion and resurrection.

BLUE: Here I would say something like this.

Blue represents *faith*. Jesus died for our sins and the rose from the dead. But, what does He expect from us? He expects us to respond in simple faith. It's not enough to just know that Jesus did this. We need to put our trust in what He did.

I would then give an illustration like the *Flying in an Airplane* illustration given under RED in the *Some Useful Illustrations* chapter.

WHITE: I would then introduce *white* this way.

So, how do we respond in faith? The Bible tells us, in Romans 10:13, *"For whosoever shall call upon the name of the Lord shall be saved."*

Blue Represents *Water Baptism*
The verse Christians usually use when blue represents water baptism is Acts 2:41.

Then they that gladly received his word were baptized: and the same day there were added unto them about three thousand souls.

Here is how I would integrate blue when it represents water baptism.

WHITE: I would wrap up *white* with an invitation to accept Christ. After they pray to accept Christ and I thank God, though prayer, what they just did, then I would introduce *blue*.

BLUE: Here is what I would say about *blue*.

Once we have asked Jesus to be our Savior, God wants us to tell other people about our decision. The best way and, frankly, the biblical way to do that is through baptism. As a matter of fact, I think the best way to look at baptism is similar to when we get married and put on a wedding ring.

When I got married, right after I said, "I do," the preacher had me put a ring on my new bride's finger and she put a ring on my finger. Now, did the ring make us married? No, our oaths made us married. The ring just told people we *were* married. If I take off the ring, am I still married? Of course I am. The oath made me married. Again, the ring just told people I was married.

Suppose I started wearing the ring a couple of months before the wedding? Would that make me married? No, the ring is a simple of my oath and I haven't taken the oath, yet.

Baptism is a lot like my wedding ring. Just like the ring doesn't make me married, baptism doesn't make me a Christian. But, again, like the ring tells people I am married, baptism tells people I am a Christian.

And, just like we want to put on a ring to tell everyone we are married to the love of our life, we should want to get baptized to identify up with God and Jesus. As a matter of fact, most people in the New Testament were baptized the same day they trusted Jesus as their only way to heaven. Acts 2:41 says, *"Then they that gladly received his word were baptized: and the same day there were added unto them about three thousand souls."*

GREEN: would then go right into *green* and talk about how we can grow in Christ.

Blue Represents the Baptism of the Holy Spirit
This is a harder one to deal with since there are so many opinions out there about the initial baptism of the Holy Spirit and the filling of the Holy Spirit. So, to be a chicken and avoid opening an entire can of worms, I am going to give some guidance on where to place *blue* when talking about the Holy Spirit but that is about all I will do here. In particular, I would put blue between *white* (accepting Christ) and *green* (growing in Christ).

Final Thoughts
No matter what colors you use to present the gospel, the most important thing is that you actually DO present the gospel. As we talked about in the first chapter of this book, only 5% of Christians have ever lead anyone to Christ. This is an appalling statistic that we MUST change. I implore you to get out there and try. Not only will you see someone

go from an eternity in hell to an eternity in haven with our Father, you will actually see real blessing come to your soul. There is nothing on this planet like the high of seeing someone come to Christ because of something you did.

CLEANING UP LOOSE ENDS

Questions?

The three boys sat down in front of Cathy at the county fair. They wanted the walking stick and Cathy was pretty sure they really didn't care about the message.

As Cathy started to talk about sin, one of the boys asked, "Why didn't God make us perfect to begin with?"

Cathy replied, "That is a good question but can I place that on the side for now and, if you'd like, we'll come back to it after I finish telling you the message of the beads?"

"Sure," they all said.

After another minute, one of the other boys asked, "Do babies go to hell for their sins?"

Again, Cathy replied, "That is a good question. But, can I place that on the side for now and, if you'd like, we'll come back to it after I finish telling you the message of the beads?"

Again, "Sure."

One more time they asked a question to get her off track.

Again she said, "That is a good question but can I place that on the side for now and, if you'd like, we'll come back to it after I finish telling you the message of the beads?"

Again they responded, "Sure."

They finally settled in and began listening to what Cathy had to say. It was only a matter of time before they bowed their heads and asked Jesus to be their Savior. Their attitudes had completely changed. They were now respectable young men with the Holy Spirit living in their hearts.

There really are only two types of questions you want to not answer: those you know the answer to and those you don't. Most questions are the devil trying to get you off track. Remember, you are there to be an evangelist not a Sunday School teacher. Get them saved then they may understand the answer. But, before the Holy Spirit gets inside them, you are fighting a losing game.

Dealing with Questions

Let's take a quick minute to look at what to do when someone asks you a question while you are presenting the message of the beads. The first thing to keep in mind is that you are there to present the Gospel and not to have a theological discussion. Chances are their question is from the devil, anyway. Gently tell them:

That is a good question but, can I place that on the side for now and, if you'd like, we'll come back to it after I finish telling you the message of the beads?

If the question is of the devil and they get saved, they'll never bring up the question again. I've never had anyone ask me their question after they trusted Christ.

Key Essentials

Of all the things that were covered in this manual, the most important for you to remember are:

Ask the "Question": "Are you 100% sure if you were to die today that you would go to heaven?"

Relate (or read) the Gospel Tract to them – to stay on track.

Pray for them to understand the importance of accepting Christ.

Ask them to trust: "If Jesus is willing to accept you just the way you are, and He is, would you be willing to trust Him as your only way to heaven?"

Remember

Pray before, during and after your event.

You are working *WITH* God – He's right there beside you. All you have to do is *GO*, God will take care of the rest.

Then saith he unto his disciples, The harvest truly is plenteous, but the labourers are few; Pray ye therefore the Lord of the harvest, that he will send forth labourers into his harvest. (Matthew 9:37-38)

SAMPLE ENCOUNTER

Just some random notes:

This is the long version. Usually it's shorter than this but I wanted to put down everything for you.

I don't usually give the Scripture references. I've included them so you can look them up to see if you are comfortable with how I used them.

Words in bold are headers for your benefit – not to be spoken.

Words in italics are also some guidelines – not to be spoken.

What I usually say:

How you start the conversation usually depends on the situation. Below I'll just assume that we are at the county fair and the adult or child I am talking to has been asked to sit down to speak to me. With Agora Evangelism Ministries, the booth is set up so that, as people walk by, they are asked if they would like to get a gift (usually a wooden yard stick with the beads attached by a leather cord on one end) with a message. If they say "Yes," then they are invited to sit down (in groups of one to five) to hear the message.

If you are talking to children you just have to simplify the illustrations a bit and make it a little shorter.

Hi, my name is Bob. How are you enjoying the fair? We're with a Christian Outreach Ministry and we are telling people the message of the beads. Do you have a church that you attend?

GOLD: As I show them the gold bead, I say something like...

The gold represents heaven. God tells us that the city in heaven is pure gold (Rev 21:18). Gold represents perfection. In heaven there is no death, no sickness, there is no disease and no sorrow. There is also no sin in heaven. Heaven is perfect. That's the way God wants it, that's the way He demands it. That is also the way we would want it. We want the place we go for eternity, the place of rest and peace, to be perfect. Anything less would be unacceptable.

And any imperfections would make heaven less than heaven. Think about baking the perfect cake. If someone came along when you weren't looking and put some chili powder in the mix, the cake wouldn't be perfect any more. Just a little imperfection and the whole thing is ruined. Heaven is like that. God can't let anything in that is less than perfect. And that's where our problem comes in.

Before I go on, I ask them...

If someone were to ask you, "Are you 100% sure, if you were to die today, that you would go to heaven?" – what would you tell them?

If they say, "Yes" without explaining why, then I ask them:

If you were standing at the gates of heaven and Jesus asked you why He should let you into His heaven, what would you say?

If they answered "no" to the first question or if they answer anything but that they are trusting in the blood of Jesus alone (or something similar) to the second question then I ask them...

Let me use the rest of the beads to show you what the Bible says so you CAN know that you will go to heaven when you die.

BLACK: I'll show them the black bead now.

God tells us that "All have sinned and come short of the glory of God." (Rom 3:23) Sin is when we do something that God doesn't like. We all have sinned. And that is why we have this black bead. It represents us and our sin.

I heard a story the other day about a grandmother who took her two grandchildren to the store. The girl behaved exceptionally well but the boy was really bad. On the way home he asked his grandmother, "Can you tell mom and dad that I behaved at the store?" Grandmother said, "I can't lie." He said, "Why not, grandma? I'm only 5 years old and I already lie pretty good."

We can all relate to that story because we know it could be true. Sin in our life is like garbage in a garbage can. If you have an egg shell in the can or a gallon milk jug, it's all still trash. It doesn't matter if it's small or large. Our sin is the same way – small or big, it's still sin and God can't let it into heaven.

As a matter of fact, the Bible says that "The wages of sin is death..." (Rom 6:23a). I have a job that I go to every day. I expect to get paid for the work I do – that is my wages and that is what I earned for the work I did. God says that the wages we deserve for our sin is death. And the Bible says it's not just physical death but it's also spiritual death. (Rev 20:14) This means that, if I were to get what I deserve for my sins, I'd have to go to hell and stay there forever and ever and ever and never get out. But God doesn't want that. He wants me to spend eternity with Him but I can't.

God wants us to be in heaven with Him. So He had to figure out a way to get us there – to a place we can't get to on our own.

RED: Now I hold the red bead in front of them.

And this brings us to the red bead. Two thousand years ago God the Son came down to take our place – to take the punishment for our sins. The Bible says, "For God so loved the world that He gave His only begotten Son, that whosoever believeth in Him should not perish but have everlasting life." (John 3:16) God wants us to be in heaven for all eternity. Our sin is keeping us out. The only way that God could get us there was if He could find someone perfect to take our place - His Son would take our punishment for us.

A movie came out a few years ago that showed all the physical suffering that Jesus went through on His way to the cross and on the cross. But this movie, as gruesome as it was, didn't come close to showing the real misery that Jesus went through. When He hung on the cross, God the Father took all the sins of the world – He took Hitler's sins, He took the terrorist's sins, He took my sins, He took your sins – He took the sins of the whole world and laid them on the shoulders of God the Son, Jesus Christ. The Bible says "God commended His love toward us, in that, while we were yet sinners, Christ died for us." (Rom 5:8) Then, on the third day He rose from the dead.

WHITE: Now I hold the white bead.

If we are sinners and Christ died for our sins, how do we take advantage of what God has already done for us? God says in the Bible that "the gift of God is eternal life through Jesus Christ." (Rom 6:23b) The Bible says this is a gift. These beads I have in my hand are mine. The leather strap and the beads have already been paid for and I can give them to whomever I choose. Even the stick they are tied to belongs to me. Now, if I want to give these beads to you, what do you have to do to get them?

Here I get them to say that all they have to do is reach out and take them.

Now that you have the beads, if I tell you that you have to clean them every week or I'll take them back, is it still a gift?

They'll say no.

If I tell you that you have to pay me a nickel every month or I'll take back the beads, then is it still a gift? Of course not. A gift is free and there is nothing you can do to pay for it or it's no longer a gift.

So, if we can't work for this gift and we can't earn this gift, how do we get it?

God says, "He that believeth on the Son hath everlasting life." (John 3:36a) What does it mean to believe? Believing means to totally trust. It's like getting on an airplane. When you want to go somewhere (say, Orlando, FL) you get on an airplane flown by a pilot you've never met, whose credentials you've never examined, to get you someplace that you want to be. You are putting your life in that pilot's hands and trusting him to get you someplace you want to be. Trusting in Jesus is similar. God is asking you to put your life in the hands of a man (Jesus) you've never met and trusting Him with your life to get you to somewhere you want to be (heaven).

After I've shown them the first four beads, then I do a quick review...

Let me ask you,

- Do you believe in a place called heaven? (*I hold up the gold bead.*)
- Do you believe that we are all sinners? (*I hold up the black bead.*)
- Do you believe that, like the Bible says, we owe a penalty for those sins? (*I still hold up the black bead.*)
- Do you believe that Jesus, God the Son, died on the cross for our sins, was buried and three days later rose from the dead? (*I hold up the red bead.*)

Now I ask them if I can pray for them. I typically pray something along the lines of...

Before I ask you my last question, may I say a little prayer for us?

Dear God, thank you for bringing us together and thank you for Mr. Jones' willingness to listen to Your word and for his honesty in telling me that he is not sure he is on his way to heaven. I pray now that You will speak to his heart about his need for Jesus as his Savior.

I don't say an Amen after this prayer, I go right into the next question – this maintains an attitude of prayer.

Then I ask them...

If Jesus is willing to accept you just the way you are, and He is, would you be willing to trust in Him as your only way to heaven?

If they say no (and they usually say yes) I try to find out why and give them a tract to take with them to read and pray about. But, if they follow the Holy Spirit this far they will usually pray to accept Christ as their Savior. Anyway, after they say yes then I say:

Okay, I'm going to lead you in a little prayer to tell God that you want to trust in Christ to get you to heaven. Just keep in mind that it's not the prayer that gets you to heaven – it's believing in your heart that Jesus died for your sins, rose from the dead and you are trusting in Him alone to get you to heaven. The prayer is just how we tell God what we believe in our hearts.

Okay, let's bow our heads. I'm going to help you pray. I'll say a few words and I want you to repeat them and mean them from your heart.

I'll say a line at a time and wait for them to repeat it.

God, I know that I am a sinner.
I know that Jesus died on the cross for my sins.
Please forgive me of my sins.
Come into my life and my heart to save me.
I ask the best I know how.
In Jesus name, Amen.

If you meant that with all your heart, shake my hand.

Now it is very important that you give them some assurance of their salvation.

There were a lot of important decisions made today – business, political, billion dollar deals could have been decided. But nothing in the whole world is more important than the decision you made just now. God says, "What shall it profit a man if he gains the whole world and loses his soul?" (Mark 8:36)

For this next part I try to open the tract to the white bead section or have my Bible or New Testament open for him to actually read.

Now, I want to share with you one more thing then I'll tell you about the green bead. The Bible says "That whosoever shall call upon the name of the Lord shall be saved." (Rom 10:13) Who do you think "whosoever" is? That's anybody in the world, that's me, that's you. Did you just call on the name of the Lord? This passage says that whosoever (that's you) shall call on the name of the Lord (that's what you just did) shall be saved. Where do you think saved people go? (They usually say heaven.) So, if you were to die tonight, where do you think you would spend eternity? (Sometimes you can even see the light turn on as they realize they are one of God's own now.)

Now notice, once you've accepted Christ as your Savior you are a child of God forever. So tomorrow, or later today, if you sin, it doesn't mean that you have to get saved all over again. If one of my daughters does something wrong she's still my daughter. If she breaks a window, she's still my daughter. If she grows up to become an international jewel thief, changes her name and moves to Africa she's still my daughter. I may get upset with her, but she'll always be my daughter.

It's the same way with our new relationship to God. By sinning, now that we are saved, we grieve the

Lord and hurt our personal fellowship with Him. But, keep in mind, we may break fellowship by sinning but we can never break son-ship. And if we do break that fellowship, all we have to do is pray and ask God to forgive us and our fellowship is restored.

I'll open the tract to the Birth certificate to have them sign and date it.

As a matter of fact, I want you to sign this spiritual Birth Certificate. (Then I usually have them read it to me.)

GREEN: Finally...

The best way to help us keep that fellowship strong is to remember the green bead. This bead stands for GROW. On the back of this tract are some ways you can grow closer to God. A good way to remember what to do, though, is remember to GROW:

G is for "Go to church." We should find a church where Bible-believing Christians gather to worship and praise God.

R stands for "Read your Bible." The only way we can know what God has for us and wants us to do is to read our Bibles. If you've never read the Bible before, I'd suggest you start with the Gospel of John. It's pretty easy reading and it will tell you the story of Jesus and His life here on earth.

O stands for "Obey God." God tells us that, when we accept what Christ did on the cross for us, the Holy Spirit comes to live in our hearts and God writes His laws on our hearts. A real miracle happened and your life will be different. Things you used to do and not think twice about will start to feel different. God is trying to mold you to be the child He wants you to be. You need to listen to that voice. You also need to talk to God every day and tell your heavenly Father what is on your mind, and seek His guidance.

W stands for "Witness." That's what I've been doing with you these past few minutes. God wants us to tell others about Him and the love He has for us.

In the Great Commission God not only tells us to win the lost, He also tells us to make disciples. We need to encourage the people we win to Christ to either join our church or (if they are too far away) to join a good Bible-believing church in their local area.

As I hand them a follow-up book, I ask them...

I'm going to give you this book to read. It will tell you about the decision you made today and what it means to be a child of God. As I said earlier, this is the most important decision you will ever make. I would love to help you celebrate by sending you a letter of encouragement or have someone from our church visit you. Would that be OK?

If they say, "Yes," then I will hand them a follow-up card and ask them to fill it out. Then I will shake their hand and welcome them to the family of God.

Congratulations and welcome to God's family. I hope we get to meet again on this side of heaven

Bob Dudley

SOME USEFUL ILLUSTRATIONS

Here are some illustrations you can use to explain the different parts of the Message of the Beads. Use the ones that fit you or discover your own. But, whatever you do, remember – it is your job to tell and explain the Gospel, it is God's job to convince them. When using illustrations it is critical to keep in mind that we should not use the illustrations to replace quoting the scriptures. God's word is what convicts the soul. Our illustrations just help us to explain the Bible truths.

GOLD: Eternal Life in Heaven

Golden Arches and the Golden Gate

I use this illustration to introduce the gold bead. It usually gets a smile (especially from the children) and it breaks the ice a bit.

The gold bead represents heaven. Now, this isn't the golden arches because that would be McDonald's. And, no matter what the kids think, that's not heaven The gold bead doesn't represent the golden gate because that would be San Francisco. And we know that's not heaven either. The Bible says that heaven is made of gold and the streets are lined with gold. The gold bead represents heaven and its perfection.

Baking a Cake

This illustration is a great transition from the gold bead to the black bead. It really shows why God can't let sin into heaven and why that is a problem for us.

Imagine trying to bake the perfect cake. You've added the exact amount of flour, the best eggs and sugar. Everything is precise to the nth degree. And, just before you put it in the oven, a small child comes by and dumps some chili pepper in the pan. Now your cake that was perfect has instantly become less than perfect. Heaven is perfect and, because of that, God can't let anything less than perfect enter. If He does, then heaven becomes less than perfect.

BLACK: Sin

Grandma

This is another fun illustration to show we are, indeed, sinners. It is a very non-threatening, non-offensive illustration because it is about a childhood situation that we can all relate to and all smile at.

Sometimes I like to tell the story about the grandmother that took her two grandchildren to the store. The granddaughter, of course, behaved like a little princess. The grandson, on the other hand, was very rambunctious. On the way home he asked his grandmother, "Will you tell mom and dad that I behaved at the store?" She said, "No, I can't lie." He looked at her with big eyes and said, "Why not, grandma? I'm only 5 years old and I already lie pretty good." We laugh at this because it rings true. Even 5-year-olds know how to sin.

Trash Can

This illustration is a good one to show that, no matter how big or small the sin is, it's all still sin.

Sin in our life is like garbage in a garbage can. If you have an egg shell in the can or a gallon milk jug its all still trash. It doesn't matter if it's small or large. Our sin is the same way – small or big, its still sin and God can't let it into heaven.

Darts

I use this illustration to show that, when we sin, we are missing the mark. No matter how good we are we can never measure up to God's perfection.

Have you ever played darts? The idea is to get the darts into the bull's eye – right smack dab in the middle. I can't have a dart board at my house because, not only would I never hit the bull's eye, I'd hardly ever hit the dart board. There'd be little dart holes all over the wall. You see, I'd miss the mark. And that is what sin is. God has given us his perfect will, His bull's eye, and when we sin we miss the mark. We are less than perfect.

Lava Flow

This is another good illustration to show that we can never reach God's perfection. One person may come closer than another. But, unless they are completely perfect, they still are not good enough.

There were two men out climbing a mountain one day when it erupted into a volcano. The lava was flowing all around them and they had no way of escape. The older of the two decided to try to jump the 10 feet to safety. He only made it about 5 feet and fell to his doom into the hot lava. The younger, more athletic, man also tried to jump. He made it further than the first man – about 8 feet. But he still fell short of reaching the other side. God tells us that, because of our sin, we all fall short of His perfection. No matter how close we think we may come we are always going to come up short.

RED: Christ's Blood

Flying in an Airplane

I first heard Curtis Hudson use this illustration. It's perfect for showing that we must trust in Christ totally and completely to get to heaven.

Have you ever flown in an airplane? When you get in the plane you turn to the right to find your seat. On the left, as you come in, is the cockpit – where the pilot sits. You've never met him, you don't know where he went to school to get his pilot's license - you don't even know if he has a pilot's license. But you are going to put your life in the hands of a man you've never met and trust him completely to get you somewhere you want to be. Trusting in Jesus is the same. You need to put your life in the hands of a man you've never met, Jesus, and trust what He did on the cross to get you someplace (heaven) that you want to be.

Free Gift of the Stick

This is a great way to use what you have at hand to make your point. Eternity is a free gift and offering the stick is a great way to show this point.

I have this walking stick that I'm going to give to you. Now, I've already paid for it and it's mine to give it to whomever I choose. I want to give it to you. What do you have to do to receive it? That's right, just reach out and take it. Now, if I tell you that you have to give me a dime every month or I'm going to take it back, is it a free gift? No, you have to pay me for it. Suppose I say you can keep it as long as you dust it off every week. Otherwise, I'll come over to your house and take it back. Now is it a free gift? Nope, you have to work for it. In order for it to be totally free there has to be no strings attached. I give it to you and it is yours forever. The gift of Christ's death on the cross is the same. There is nothing you can do to pay for it or work for it. The price has already been paid and all you have to do is reach out and take it.

Thief on the Cross

The power of this illustration is that it is a true story right from the Bible. It also shows the entire plan of salvation in one illustration. This is a long illustration but one well worth using to sum up all that you've talked about up to this point.

Let me give you an illustration right out of the Bible. When Jesus was on the cross He was crucified between two thieves – one on the left and one on the right.

The one on the left said, "If you're the Son of God get

us off the cross." He wasn't concerned about going to heaven or spiritual things – he simply wanted to get off the cross and get free.

But the man on the right hand side said, "Lord, remember me when Thou comest into Thy kingdom." That's all he said, "...remember me when Thou comest into Thy kingdom."

Jesus said to him, "Today shalt thou be with Me in paradise."

Now this fellow has never been baptized, never joined a church, certainly didn't lead a good life. But he realized four things – the same four things I'm saying to you.

- He knew, #1, that he was a sinner. That's why he was on the cross – he was a thief.
- He knew, #2, that he was going to die. Anybody that went to the cross, they died. This happened to be Passover and if they were not dead by 6 PM soldiers would come with a sledge hammer and break their legs – there would be no means of support and they would suffocate to death. So, he knew he was going to die physically. But he also knew that he was going out to eternity without hope unless he did something about it.
- He knew, #3, that Jesus was the answer to his problem. He called Him Lord. He said, "Lord," remember me when Thou comest into Thy kingdom."
- Finally, #4, he recognized Jesus was the Son of God. Again, he called Him Lord. He said, "Lord,

remember me when Thou comest into Thy kingdom."

And Jesus said to him, "TODAY shalt thou be with Me in paradise." That's why the Bible says, "Whosoever shall call upon the name of the Lord shall be saved." (Rom 10:13)

Taking Your Brother's Punishment

This is a good illustration to help children understand the substitutionary death of Christ for our sins.

Suppose your brother decides to throw a rock through the living room window. Of course your parents are a little upset.

Your dad decides to put him on restriction for a week — no TV, no video games, no phone, no friends, no fun.

He apologizes but the punishment has to be paid.

Because you love your brother you jump up and say, "I love my brother and I want him to be free. I'll take his punishment for him, I'll go on restriction." You would do that for him, wouldn't you?

Even though you are willing to take your brother's punishment, even though you ran into your room and jumped on the bed, it doesn't count until he agrees to accept your sacrifice, it doesn't count as a replacement for his restriction.

WHITE: A Cleansed Heart

Falling in the Mud

I find that cute illustrations involving children usually are the most non-threatening and easiest way to get your point across without offending the person you're trying to save.

Imagine taking a small child to church one Sunday morning. On the way to the car she falls into a puddle of mud and gets filthy. You take her inside, wash her body, change her clothes and comb out her hair. When she gets to church everyone thinks she is perfectly clean. As far as they can tell, she never got dirty. That's the way it is when God forgives us of our sins. We are washed clean and you could never tell that, in God's eyes, we were ever dirty.

GREEN: Christian Growth and Assurance
GROW

A little girl at a county fair actually showed me this one. I've used it ever since. It's easy to memorize and a great way to encourage the new Christian to GROW.

One way to look at the green bead is with an acrostic:

G – go to church
R – read your Bible
O – obey God
W – witness (that's what we are doing right now – telling others about Jesus' love)

A Log out of a Fireplace

I heard this one when I was a young Christian many years ago. But it's still good today.

Have you ever seen a roaring fire? When all the logs are burning together they put out a lot of heat and a lot of light. But, if you take one log and set it on the side, soon it will become dark and cold. You need to keep it with the other logs to keep it warm. Our walk with God is the same — we need to be with other Christians to help us grow and stay close to God.

International Jewel Thief

This one usually gets a chuckle and it's a great way to talk about what it means to be a child of God.

Once you accept Jesus as your Savior, you are a child of God (John 1:12) and no one can ever take that away from you — not even you. Over the next few days you are going to sin, you might even sin sometime today. But that doesn't mean you are no longer going to heaven.

Do you have any children? Well, suppose one of them breaks a window. Is he still your child? Of course he is. You may be upset with him but he is still your child. Suppose he steals a car — still your child? If he robs a bank — still your child? Becomes an international jewel thief and moves to Africa — still your child? You may get upset with him but, no matter what he does after he has become your child, he will always be your child. You share DNA. As a child of God you share God's DNA.

Microwave Clear Button

This is a great illustration to explain what it means to be forgiven by God of the sins we confess.

Have you ever put in the wrong time when you wanted to heat something up in the microwave? What do you do? You hit the CLEAR button. Then you get a do-over. God gives us a clear button in I John 1:9 - If we confess our sins, he is faithful and just to forgive us our sins, and to cleanse us from all unrighteousness. All we have to do when we fail is humble ourselves before God and ask for His forgiveness. We get a do-over – God pushes the CLEAR button and we regain fellowship with Him.

IMPORTANT NOTE:

Never forget that it is the Holy Spirit that brings conviction to the heart through the hearing of the gospel (Rom 10:17). Whatever illustrations you use are to help the person you are talking to understand what God is saying to them. The illustrations should never be used as a substitute for God's word.

TESTIMONIES

I Didn't Know That

The Eastern Sports and Outdoor Show was this last week. There was an evangelism booth at the show and this last Saturday our church (Granite Baptist, Glen Burnie, MD) ran the booth. The booth is set up with a sign that reads "Free Gift with a Message." There are about a dozen chairs in the booth and 4 or 5 soul winners – people trained to lead others to Christ. People come in and sit down to get a walking stick (a square yard stick with a little leather strap on one end holding colored beads – gold, black, red, white, and green). They have to sit down and hear the gospel in order to get the stick. We usually have a chance to give a clear presentation of the gospel to anywhere from a few hundred to over a thousand people a day at a medium-sized fair.

Well, we made it to the Sports Fair this last weekend – even with the snow. It was not as busy as last year at the evangelism booth (I heard a lot of people stayed home because of the weather). But we still saw a lot of decisions for Christ on Saturday – over 140 people prayed to ask Jesus to be their Savior.

I know every decision is sweet to God. And, every once in a while, He gives us a taste of how sweet they are. In particular, I'm thinking of a gentleman Cathy was able to lead to Christ on Saturday afternoon. Cathy was sitting in the back of the booth when a couple walked in to hear the message of the beads and to get their free walking stick. As they sat down and Cathy engaged them in conversation it became very apparent the young man (in his late 20s) was mentally handicapped and the lady was probably his nurse or aide and she was already saved.

As Cathy went through the plan of salvation she got to the part where she talks about Christ's death, burial and resurrection. When she told him that Christ had actually risen from the dead the young man's eyes got big as saucers. He said, "No way, I didn't know that!" and "Really?!" and "Wow, I never knew Jesus rose from the dead. No one ever told me that before!"

Before Cathy asks people if they would like to trust in Jesus as their only way to heaven, she does a little review to make sure they understand everything she has told them. She asked him if he knew he had done some sins in his life.

He said, "Yes."

She asked him if he understood there was a punishment for his sins.

Again, he said "Yes."

She asked him if he understood that Jesus paid for those sins on the cross.

Once more he said, "Yes."

Then she asked if he believed that Jesus rose from the dead.

He said, "No way!"

She told him she could show him in the Bible where it said that.

He said, "Oh, I believe you now. Just, no one ever told me that before. I never knew that. But now I know because you told me. I know Jesus rose from the dead."

Cathy held his hand and prayed that he would be saved today. She then asked him if he would like to ask Jesus to save him so he would go to heaven some day. He said, "Of course!" Then he asked Jesus to be his Savior.

As Cathy told me later about this young man, it got me to thinking. How many times a day do we overlook talking to someone about eternity? How many people have we had a chance to talk to and we were able to make up some excuse why it wasn't the right time to witness to them? How many Christians did God send across the path of that young man and they thought, "He's too slow to understand, he just wouldn't get it?"

It says, in Luke 10:2 - *Therefore said he unto them, "The harvest truly is great, but the labourers are few: pray ye therefore the Lord of the harvest, that he would send forth labourers into his harvest.*"

Every day there are people, in our neighborhoods, who go into an eternity without the Savior. How many people do we come across every day that "… never knew Jesus rose from the dead." And they never will know unless we tell them. *Pray ye therefore the Lord of the harvest, that he would send forth laborers into his harvest.* And pray that WE would be those laborers.

Dan at the Fair

I was working at the evangelism booth on Saturday morning. I was standing in front of our booth area, off to one side, talking to a young couple. As I was wrapping up, I noticed a family from our church approaching the booth — a mom, dad and two young daughters (grade school age).

At first I thought they were there to help with the personal evangelism. Then I noticed they were walking around the booth (we weren't very busy) and were talking very excitedly among themselves.

After the couple left I was working with I turned to the family and said, "Hi, Dan. What's up?"

His wife chimed in (huge smile on her face) and told me that he was showing them "where it happened."

Then it hit me. On Friday Pastor Frazier had told me that Thursday night Dan was working at the booth and, not only did he talk to someone about Jesus for the first time in his life, he actually had led four people to Christ that night. He had brought his family to the fair just to show them where he had led his first people to Christ.

I asked her if she was talking about the miracles on Thursday night that her husband was a part of.

Nodding her head, "yes", she told me that, when he got home on Thursday night, they stayed up until way past midnight recounting every detail and every miracle of the night. Dan couldn't get a word in edgewise.

With tears in her eyes she told me about each of the people that are going to heaven now because her husband stepped way out of his comfort zone and was willing to talk about the closest thing to his heart.

As they walked away from the booth arm in arm, each holding a daughter's hand, I was sure their feet never touched the ground.

A Teenage Attitude

I think one of the traps you can fall into when you do a lot of witnessing and see a lot of results is thinking that you can tell who is going to get saved or not when you are talking to people. I had a humbling experience concerning this at a fair in Ohio. A teenaged girl sat down in front of me to hear the message of the beads so she could get her walking stick.

It was obvious to me as I talked to her about the fair that she was only there to get the stick and she was tolerating the message. I told her we were from the Christian Outreach ministry (pointing to the sign at the back of the booth). I asked her if she attended church anywhere. She said, "Not really." I asked her if she was 100% sure, if something should happen to her, that she would go to heaven. She mumbled something akin to "whatever" as she rolled her eyes and looked away to watch the people walking by.

I went ahead with the gospel anyway. I quoted her the verses of the Romans' Road, but I really didn't put my heart into it. I had several illustrations I had been using throughout the week and I left most of them out. At the end of the gospel presentation I asked her if I could pray for her. With a nod of her head, I bowed my head and asked God, aloud, that He touch her heart and show her that she needed to trust His Son as her Savior. Then I asked her if she would like to trust Jesus as her only way to heaven.

She told me, "sure".

So I led her through the sinner's prayer. Only she didn't say it out loud. Usually people ask me if they have to say it out loud and I tell them they are talking to God and they can pray silently. But she never asked so I just assumed that she didn't even pray.

When I looked up after the prayer I realized why she couldn't pray aloud. She had huge tears streaming down her face and she was crying uncontrollably. I held both her hands for about 5 minutes. When she was able to talk again she said, "God loves me."

It's not about us. It's about God's holy word and God's Holy Spirit. We just tell the gospel. God uses it to save and change lives. I pray that I never, ever, take God's power and the power of His word for granted when it comes to talking to lost souls.

How Do You Get One of Those Sticks?

Marcus and I were in Alabama working in a booth handing out free walking sticks with a gospel message. While there we became good friends with Roger. Roger was there selling his wares. But in his spare time he had an evangelism ministry so he was pretty interested in what we were doing.

On the second day Roger came over during his break hoping to watch Marcus present the gospel a few times – maybe pick up a pointer or two. While he was standing in the aisle waiting for Marcus to finish with a group of teen agers he felt a tap on his shoulder. It was Steve, an old high school buddy he hadn't seen in 20 years.

Roger asked him what he was doing there. Steve said he had been walking around the show and saw several people carrying walking sticks. He heard he could get one at this booth and wondered what he had to do to get one.

Roger, recalling that he and his friends had witnessed to Steve for years in school in vain said, "All you have to do is listen to that guy for a few minutes and you get the stick for free."

Steve said, "I can do that."

After the teenagers left Roger and Steve sat down in front of Marcus. Marcus asked Steve, "Are you 100% sure, if you were to die today, that you would go to heaven?"

Steve wasn't sure and Marcus had the opportunity to show him, through accepting Jesus as his Savior, he could be sure. Steve bowed his head and asked Jesus to come into his heart.

Roger spent the rest of the day calling all his friends and telling them about the harvest he had seen that day from a seed they had planted 20 years ago. Never, never give up on your friend and loved ones – you never know when they will finally see the light.

God Let Me Watch as He Got Saved

I was standing outside a booth at a sports show in Alabama trying to get people to come in to hear a free (gospel) message and get a walking stick. Two large hunter-type manly men came up to me to see what it was all about. They didn't want to take time to sit down so I just talked to them in the aisle.

After a few minutes it was obvious that one of them knew for sure that Jesus was his Savior and he was on his way to heaven. The other man was just as unsure about where he was going to go after he died. I had the joy of leading him to the Lord.

After going through some assurance with him about his decision to trust in Jesus as his only way to heaven he left. But the other man stood there at my side. I thought that was pretty strange. I was sure they were together. So I looked over at him to see what he might want and this man that was at least 6'3" had huge tears running down his face.

He told me that he had been driving his friend to work every day for the last six months and tried to witness to him every day. And every day he went home disappointed that his buddy was still lost. Today, he told me, he got to see all of that hard work come to completion. He got to see his friend come to the Lord. He grabbed me and lifted me off the ground in a big bear hug and walked away with a spring in his step.

William is Home Now

I was working at a booth in North Carolina. It was a Thursday and three gentlemen came in to hear the message of the beads and get a free walking stick. It turned out that of the three, one was the grandfather, one was the father and the other was the son (all three adults). I went through the gospel and found out that the grandfather and the son knew that they were saved and on their way to heaven. The father (William) wasn't sure.

William's son turned to him and said, "Dad, we never know how much time we have. You should accept Christ as your Savior."

William was only 49-years-old but he agreed with his son. He bowed his head and asked Jesus to come into his heart.

That night at home William told his Christian wife what he had done. She was overjoyed with the news. He told her that it was about time he went to church with them and, on Sunday, he did just that. William went to church and told the pastor that he had realized he was a sinner and needed Jesus in his heart. He told the pastor that he took care of that on Thursday.

Monday William went to work and came home. Tuesday, same as every day, he went to work. The only difference was, he never made it home. On the way home from work William died of a heart attack. His funeral was on Thursday – one week after he asked Jesus to come into his heart. William is home with the Lord now. Are you 100% sure that, if you died today, you would go to heaven?

ARE *YOU* 100% SURE ABOUT HEAVEN?

I have taught evangelism classes all over the world. From Washington, DC to Nairobi, Kenya. One of the most precious memories I have, almost every time I teach, is seeing someone in the class realize they have never made that commitment to have a life in Jesus and they take care of it right there in the classroom.

That is why I ask, every time I lead a class on evangelism: Are YOU 100% sure, if something happened to you today, that you would go to heaven? Maybe you have been in church all of your life. Maybe you are even working in a ministry in your church. But, upon reflection, you just can't recall ever putting your trust in Jesus as your only way to heaven. If this is the case, if you are not sure about heaven, please read this carefully.

There's one problem that we have to deal with before we can get to heaven and that problem is us. You see, the Bible says, *"For all have sinned and come short of the glory of God."* (Rom 3:23) We've talked about this some throughout the book but, the bottom line, all of us have sinned. If I am old enough to write this and you are old enough to read it then I think we are BOTH old enough to understand that *we have sinned*, that we have done some things that God does not like. Haven't we?

The Bible also says, *"The wages of sin is death."* (Rom 6:23a) What this means is, no matter how much we want to be in heaven, we're not allowed to go. **We can't get into heaven with our sins.**

Fortunately, that's not the end of the story. God sent His Son, Jesus, to the earth 2,000 years ago to die for our sins. They nailed Him to a cross and put a spear in His side. He died. Next, they put Him in a tomb. Then, 3 days later on Easter, what happened to Him? That's right, He rose from the dead. Do you know that He is the only one in history to ever die and 3 days later rise himself from the dead?

The Bible says about this that, *"God proved His love to us in that, while we were sinners, Christ died for us."* (Rom 5:8) **Jesus died for me and for you and for the entire world. He died for everyone.** The Bible tells us that, *"The gift of God is eternal life through Jesus Christ our Lord."* (Rom 6:23b) Eternal life is a free gift for everyone! But, how do we get this free gift?

Like any gift, eternal life isn't really ours until we reach out and take it, until we accept it, receive it. The Bible says the way we accept His gift of eternal life is just to ask for it. The Bible says, *"Whosoever shall call upon the name of the Lord shall be saved."* (Rom 10:13) What this simply means is **there must be a moment in your life where you personally decide that Jesus died for your sins and rose from the dead and that you are going to trust Him as your only way to heaven.** Now, let me ask you a really serious question, a question you may recall from earlier in the book. **If Jesus is willing to accept you just the way you are, and He is, would you be willing to accept Him and trust Him as your only way to heaven?**

Let's tell God that you want to trust Jesus. When I was 14 someone asked me if I wanted to trust Jesus and I didn't know how to tell God that I wanted to do that. He helped me say a prayer to God. I want to help you with that same prayer. Keep in mind, it's not the prayer that lets you put your trust in Jesus, it's what you believe in your heart. The prayer is just telling God what you want to do, that you want to trust in His Son, Jesus.

So, pray this prayer, and mean it:

God, I know that I am a sinner.
I know that Jesus died on the cross for my sins.
Please forgive me of my sins.
Come into my life and my heart to save me.
I ask the best I know how.
In Jesus name, Amen.

Now, I want to share one more thing with you.

The Bible says *"That whosoever shall call upon the name of the Lord shall be saved."* (Rom 10:13) Who do you think "whosoever" is? That's anybody in the world, that's me, that's you. Did you just call on the name of the Lord?

This passage says that whosoever (that's you) shall call on the name of the Lord (that's what you just did) shall be saved. So, according to God's Word, are you a saved person or a lost person? That's right, you are a saved person. Where do you think saved people go? That's right, to heaven. So, if you were to die tonight, you would spend eternity in heaven!

Do me a favor. This is the most important decision you will ever make. I would love to celebrate it with you. Can you drop me a letter or an email letting me know that you've trusted Jesus as your Savior? Here's my contact information:

Bob Dudley
Executive Director

Lura B Walker Foundation
55 Christians Dr
Hanover, PA 17331

BobDudley@EverydayEvangelism.org

Gold Represents Heaven

Bob Dudley

SALVATION BRACELETS

Are you going on a short-term missions trip and you don't know how to share Jesus in a life changing way?

Is your church having a block party and you want to have an effective evangelism tent for all the children in the neighborhood?

The salvation bracelets are for you! You need the Color Kit!

We have Color Kits for your evangelism needs. The kits come in 2 sizes: you can get the 100 pack or, if you plan to reach a lot of people, you can get the 1,000 pack.

Each pack comes with rawhide bracelets, gold, black, red, white and green colored beads, and "Do You Know?" tracts for 100 (or, for the larger kit, 1,000) bracelets.

If you are not sure how many you need for your particular event, send us an email telling us the name and type of event, how many days you will be there, and the size of the volunteer team you have. We would be happy to help you plan your needs.

Color Kit:

Comes in 100 pack and Jumbo (1,000!)

… is available online at

https://SquareUp.com/store/Everyday-Evangelism

This is Madison Strempek's first book AND it is a #1 bestseller. AND, if that wasn't enough, Madison wrote this book when she was 10-years-old!

When Madison was trying to learn how to cope with her daddy going to prison, she could not find any books out there written for a child BY a child. She told her mom, "If there aren't any books for me, I'll just write one myself. Children need to know they are not alone."

Everyone Makes Mistakes: Living With My Daddy In Jail is the result of that effort. Here is what people are saying about this VERY special young lady:

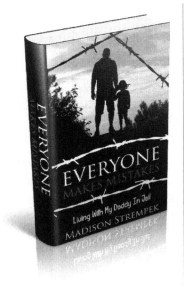

"*Your voice is important, and I trust you will keep working hard to pursue your dreams. I want you to hold on to the optimism and resolve that have brought you this far, and I am confident you will continue to do great things.*"
President of the United States of America, Barack Obama

"*Your intro of Attorney General, Loretta Lynch was 100%, Madison. Thanks for speaking up for your dad and other kids of incarcerated parents.*"
Author of "Orange is the New Black," Piper Kerman

Everyone makes Mistakes:

Living With My Daddy In Jail ...

... is available online at

www.Amazon.com

www.BarnesAndNoble.com

In 2003 I decided to leave my job as an astro-nautical engineer (or, as my mom called me, a rocket scientist) and become, of all things, an evangelist. It was an interesting transition and a very eye opening journey. This #1 bestselling book is a result of that journey. I first thought an evangelist was the church "officer" responsible for leading people to Christ. I soon discovered the evangelist (and ALL church leaders) are responsible for teaching other Christians how to lead people to Christ (see chapter three) and it is the av-erage Christian's responsibility to lead others to Christ, to evangelize.

As I traveled around the world, I met hun-dreds of well meaning and sincere pastors who had all the heart they could have but had no real guidance on how to grow their church the way the disciples in the New Tes-tament grew the church. I began to teach them and retrain them to have the heart of God, to have a heart for the lost. We began to refocus their ministries from the earthly to the eternal. It wasn't long before these pastors saw their churches double and triple in size with born again believers.

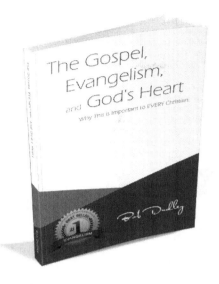

What I have tried to capture in this book are all the questions and discussions we have had with these pastors - both in the classroom and sitting up late at night over coffee and diet cola. I hope, as you read this book, you discover a deeper apprecia-tion and understanding for the gospel, evangelism and God's heart.

The Gospel, Evangelism, and God's Heart:
Why This is Important to EVERY Christians ...

... is available online at
www.Amazon.com
www.BarnesAndNoble.com

EVERYDAY EVANGELISM

Everyday Evangelism is a 12-week training course for personal evangelism repeated 4 times annually at your church. It is a program designed to energize and train the lay people in your church to make them enthusiastic soul winners. *Everyday Evangelism* teaches personal evangelism using:

♦ On-the-job training (2-by-2 soul winning/ mentoring)

♦ Bible verse memorization

♦ Classroom lecture

♦ Reading assignments (Bible and textbook)

You start out with just two people – a mentor and a trainee. After the first 12-week session, the two of you are mentors and you bring on two more people – four going out every week to share the gospel. This continues every 12 weeks – 4 times a year. After two years you have the potential for 256 people going out every week to witness. Practically, we are seeing at least 100 going out (some only do one session, some are not comfortable being mentors, some move on to their ministry while using what they learned in *Everyday evangelism*).

With *Everyday Evangelism*, you are not just "buying a kit", you are investing in a continuing partnership to train and equip your staff and your people to change the world around them and grow the Kingdom of God.

We take the fear out of evangelism. We do this through a mentorship program that pairs experienced soul winners (who do ALL the talking) with the Christian just learning. We teach Christians a plan, we teach them what to say – how to start a conversation, how to lovingly present the gospel, how to invite someone to accept Christ.

We multiply the church's time for evangelism. We show you how to engage the entire congregation to fulfill the Great Commission. You no longer will have to depend on "professional" Christians to spread the Good News.

DIRECTORS' COLLEGE

We reach your entire Jerusalem. By engaging your entire congregation, the church's evangelistic reach will extent to their loved ones, friends, co-workers and acquaintances.

We integrate evangelism into any church program. We show you how to tie evangelism into every one of the church's ministries. From Sunday school to vacation Bible school, from feeding the hungry to building shelters, from block parties to short term mission trips, we show you how to turn every opportunity into a gospel outreach. Our goal is growing God's Kingdom - an unintended consequence of this is massive church growth.

If Everyday Evangelism looks like something your church can use, please:

visit us at www.EverydayEvangelism.org

Or

Contact us at Contact@EverydayEvangelism.org

Or

Visit our sales page directly...

Everyday Evangelism Directors' College:

Live Event OR At-Home Study

... is available online at

https://SquareUp.com/store/Everyday-Evangelism

ABOUT THE AUTHOR

Bob Dudley is a retired Air Force Officer and currently serves as the Executive Director and Chairman of the Board of the *Lura B Walker Foundation (LBW)*. As the head of *LBW*, Bob is involved in several aspects of evangelism. *LBW* is helping to train pastors to set up personal evangelism programs in their churches throughout the United States and around the world using the *Everyday Evangelism* program. *LBW* is also involved in evangelism crusades and pastoral training in third world countries. Bob currently lives in Hanover, PA with his wife. He has four daughters, two sons-in-law and two very precious granddaughters - Madison and Bliss.

36148619R00061

Made in the USA
Middletown, DE
26 October 2016